W9-BJE-995

ALFRED HITCHCOCK and
The Three Investigators in

The Mystery of the
SHRINKING HOUSE

by WILLIAM ARDEN

Cover illustration by Charles Liese

SCHOLASTIC INC.
New York Toronto London Auckland Sydney

ISBN 0-590-30327-9

12 11 10 9 8 7 6 5 4 3   7 8 9/8 0 1/9

Contents

A FEW WORDS FROM
ALFRED HITCHCOCK

When I first met the trio of lads who call
themselves The Three Investigators, I foolishly promised to introduce their most inter-
esting cases. Little did I realize how prolific
the lads would be! As you will see, I did my
best to avoid introducing this case — but the
boys foiled me. So I will do my duty, and pro-
ceed with yet another introduction to The
Three Investigators.

The members of this intrepid junior detective firm are Jupiter Jones, Pete Crenshaw,
and Bob Andrews. All three reside in the
town of Rocky Beach, California, a few
miles from Hollywood. Jupiter is the brains
of the firm. Pete provides the brawn. And

Bob, the most studious of the three, is in charge of research.

Together the three lads are a formidable team. They have outwitted the cleverest of crooks and survived the most terrifying situations. In their newest case they are asked to track down the missing possessions of a dead artist. A simple enough assignment — but one that leads them into strange byways of mystery and intrigue.

Now you know enough to begin reading the story . . . if you dare.

Alfred Hitchcock

A FIGURE IN BLACK

"Uncle Titus!" Jupiter Jones cried. "Look over there!"

The truck from The Jones Salvage Yard had just stopped in the driveway of the old house in Remuda Canyon on the outskirts of Rocky Beach. Jupiter and his friend Pete Crenshaw were sitting in the truck cab with Uncle Titus Jones.

"What?" Uncle Titus said, startled. "Look where, Jupiter?"

"There! On the side of the house!"

Jupiter pointed into the twilight. A black shape seemed to hang halfway up the side of the big old frame house in the canyon.

1

"I don't see a thing, Jupiter Jones," Uncle Titus said.

"Gosh," Pete said, "neither do I, Jupe."

Jupiter stared. The figure in black was gone. One minute it had been on the side of the house, then it had disappeared into thin air! Or had it been there at all?

"I'm sure I saw someone!" Jupiter said. "Someone all in black on the side of the house!"

Uncle Titus looked dubiously at the big frame house. The canyon walls cast strange, eerie shadows on the isolated house and the small cottage near it. All seemed quiet and peaceful.

"You probably saw a shadow, Jupe," said Uncle Titus.

"Canyon shadows sure play funny tricks," Pete agreed.

"No," Jupiter insisted, "I saw someone all in black, and I think he went into the house through a window!"

Uncle Titus hesitated. He knew that his stocky nephew had a great deal of imagination, and he hated to raise a false alarm. But he also knew that Jupiter was usually right.

"All right, come on then," Uncle Titus said. "We'd better tell Professor Carswell what you saw."

The two boys followed Uncle Titus up an overgrown walk to the front door of the big house. It was an old house from the last century, with wooden towers, many peaks and gables, columns holding up the porch, and a massive front door.

The man who answered their knocking was tall and thin, with very deep shadowed eyes. He wore a rumpled tweed jacket even in July, and carried a thick book in some foreign language.

"Professor Carswell?" Uncle Titus asked.

The Professor smiled. "You must be Mr. Jones from the salvage yard. Come in. What I have to sell —"

Uncle Titus interrupted, "I don't mean to alarm you, Professor, but my nephew here insists that he saw a figure all in black climbing up the side of your house a moment ago."

"Someone climbing up this house?" The Professor blinked at the boys and Uncle Titus. "You must be mistaken."

"No, sir," Jupiter said urgently, "I'm certain of what I saw. Do you have anything valuable a burglar would want?"

"I'm afraid not, young man. Absolutely nothing," Professor Carswell said. "Still, if you say you saw something, I'm sure you did. Only I can't imagine . . . ah! Of course! You must have seen my son up to one of his games. He has a black cowboy outfit, and try as I may I can't seem to convince Hal that doors are better entrances than windows."

Professor Carswell smiled again, and Uncle Titus nodded.

"Of course that's it. I know how boys are, yessir," the owner of the salvage yard said.

"How old is your son, sir?" Jupiter asked.

"A little younger than you, I guess, but taller. As tall as your friend there." The Professor nodded to Pete.

"The person I saw was much bigger," Jupiter said firmly.

"Ah?" Professor Carswell looked skeptically at Jupiter. "Very well, young man. We'll see if your burglar is in the house."

The Professor led them through the downstairs rooms of the big old house. Many of the rooms were empty and closed off.

"A professor of languages can't really afford a house like this these days," the Professor said sadly. "My ancestors were wealthy ship captains who brought goods here from the East. They built this house. Now only myself and my son remain. A cousin left the place to us a year ago. We closed off most of the rooms in this house,

4

and rented out the old caretaker's cottage to make ends meet."

They found nothing in the downstairs rooms, and went upstairs. Most of the rooms upstairs were also empty, and they saw no sign of an intruder. Jupiter studied all the rooms.

"There's not much to steal," he admitted.

"You sound disappointed," said the Professor.

"Jupe likes mysteries," Pete said. "Only there sure isn't any burglar around here."

"Professor Carswell's son isn't in the house, either," Jupiter pointed out thoughtfully. "I know I saw someone. You called Uncle Titus to sell some items to the salvage yard. Is there something valuable among them?"

"I wish there were," Professor Carswell said. "But they're only what poor old Mr. Cameron had when he died a month ago in our cottage. The contents of two suitcases, and some of his amateur paintings. Old Cameron was something of a recluse. He owned little, and couldn't even pay his rent the last few months. I hope to recover a few dollars by selling his meager possessions to your uncle."

"Recluses sometimes have hidden valuables," Jupiter said.

Professor Carswell smiled. "You sound like a detective."

"We are detectives!" Pete blurted out. "Show him, Jupe!"

Jupiter produced a business card, on which was printed:

THE THREE INVESTIGATORS

"We Investigate Anything"

? ? ?

First Investigator.....Jupiter Jones
Second Investigator..Peter Crenshaw
Records and Research..Bob Andrews

"Well, well, very impressive," Professor Carswell said. "I'm quite sorry there is nothing here to investigate, boys. It must have been the canyon shadows you saw."

The Professor had hardly stopped speaking when they heard a cry:

"Help! Help!"

They all froze. Professor Carswell listened, and suddenly turned pale.

"Help!" The cry came from outside. "Dad!"

"That's my son, Hal!" Professor Carswell exclaimed. "Come on!"

The Professor ran down the stairs and out the door with the boys and Uncle Titus right behind him. In the canyon twilight the cry came again — from the small cottage off to their left.

"Help!"

JUPITER IS RIGHT—
AND WRONG!

Professor Carswell raced across the lawn of the big house toward the small cottage, with Uncle Titus and Pete close behind him, and the overweight Jupiter puffing in the rear. Breathlessly they ran under the patched porch awning of the cottage and burst into a small living room. The room was sparsely furnished — and empty!

"Harold!" Professor Carswell called out in alarm.

"Dad!" a voice cried. "Help!"

The voice came from the tiny bedroom of the cottage. Pete and Uncle Titus followed the Professor into it. They saw a narrow cot, a chair, and a large bureau that had been knocked over. A thin boy lay on the floor half under the bureau. Professor Carswell hurried to him.

"I'm okay, Dad," the boy said. "I just can't get out."

Together Professor Carswell, Pete, and Uncle Titus heaved the heavy bureau off Hal Carswell. The boy stood up and brushed himself off.

"I heard a noise in here, Dad," Hal explained, "so I came in to look. There was someone all in black — and masked. When I yelled, he pushed the bureau over on me and ran out the back way!"

"Jupe was right!" Pete exclaimed. "He did see a man in black — but the man must have been coming *out* of your house, not going in! Jupe..."

Pete looked all around the bedroom, and out in the small living room. Jupiter was nowhere in the cottage.

"Jupiter Jones!" Uncle Titus called out.

"Gosh," Pete gulped. "He was right behind us when we ran out of the house. Where could he be?"

Professor Carswell turned to his son. "You say that would-be burglar ran out the back? Did he have a weapon, Hal?"

"I didn't see any — "

Once again they all froze as a cry broke the twilight outside the cottage. "Aggghhhhhhhhhhhh!"

Professor Carswell whirled. "That sounds as if it came from the barranca in back! Maybe someone fell in!"

"Is it a deep barranca?" Uncle Titus asked nervously.

"No, but deep enough to injure someone," Professor Carswell said. "Follow me."

The tall Professor quickly led them behind the cottage, where they crashed through the thick chaparral and live oaks in the lengthening shadows of the outlying canyon. They stopped abruptly at the edge of a narrow, steep-sided gully about ten feet deep. It ran across the canyon, curving away out of sight in both directions. Its bottom was strewn with heavy rocks and eroded trees.

There was no sign of Jupiter or anyone else.

"Look!" Pete said.

A dark stain was on some rocks below and to the right. The four of them scrambled down the steep sides to stand over the darkened rocks. Pete touched the stain. It was wet.

"Blood," the Second Investigator said, and gulped.

When Pete and the others had rushed into the cottage earlier, Jupiter had been far behind. He saw the black-garbed figure running from behind the cottage toward the heavy chaparral at the rear of the property.

The stocky First Investigator realized that no one else had seen the fleeing intruder. The man was sure to escape if Jupiter took the time to warn the others in the cottage. He hesitated for only a second, then turned and pursued the running figure.

Jupiter was unable to get a good look at the man before he vanished into the heavy brush and dusty oaks. Panting, the stout First Investigator reached the thick underbrush — just as he heard the cry ahead. There was a crashing, the sound of something sliding and falling, and then a loud thud and groaning cry.

Jupiter slipped through the dense chaparral to the edge of a narrow barranca. In the shadowed gloom at the bottom of the steep little gully, the black figure staggered up and limped off along the barranca to the right. The man was dragging his left leg.

Jupiter slid down, and at the bottom of the barranca he found blood on some rocks. A trail of blood led off to the right. Jupiter followed the trail cautiously. The gully was the perfect place for an ambush if the intruder knew he was being followed.

A car door slammed up ahead, and a car motor started. Jupiter began to run. A little way ahead the barranca came out into the main canyon road, which looped back along the side of the Carswell property before turning in the direction of Rocky Beach. By the time Jupiter reached the road, the taillights of the car were vanishing toward town.

Pete was still staring at the blood on the rocks at the bottom of the barranca when he heard someone coming. Uncle Titus heard it, too.

"Down, Peter!" he said. "Everyone . . . !"

They all crouched in the shadows of the barranca, ready to leap on the intruder.

Jupiter came around the curve in the gully.

"Jupe!" Pete cried. "What happened?"

"I chased the intruder," Jupiter said, "but I lost him."

"Jupiter Jones!" Uncle Titus exploded. "You should know better than to try to capture a thief by yourself!"

"I didn't try to capture him, Uncle Titus. I just followed to try to see his face, but it was dark, and he had a car."

Professor Carswell shook his head. "I can't understand what he wanted here. All I can imagine is that he made a mistake. There *are* wealthy people in these big canyon houses, and he must have simply picked the wrong house. Well, whatever, perhaps we should get to business, Mr. Jones?"

They all went back to the cottage. Professor Carswell switched on lights and took two old leather suitcases from the bedroom closet. In one were clothes — an old-fashioned dress suit, a gray flannel suit, and several shirts, ties, and pairs of socks. In the other were some paints, a stuffed owl, a small statue of Venus, a pair of large binoculars, and a box of silver forks, knives, and spoons.

"Old Joshua acted rough, and never wore anything but a sweat shirt and a pair of old trousers," Professor Carswell said. "But I could see he was well educated, and he always used his silver when he ate. Yet in the seven months he was here, all he did was sit out on the lawn in our canvas chair and sketch. At night he painted all the time. See?"

The Professor took a canvas covering off a pile in the corner, revealing twenty paintings.

They were all pictures of the cottage and grounds. In some, the cottage was seen from very close-up, while in others it was so far away that all you could see was the striped porch awning with its patches.

"They're not bad," Uncle Titus said. His eyes gleamed as he looked around at the suitcases, the silver cutlery, and the paintings. There was nothing Uncle Titus enjoyed more than buying things to sell in his junkyard. His wife, Jupiter's Aunt Mathilda, frequently complained about the outlandish items he found. But Uncle Titus was always convinced that a buyer would turn up. Usually he was right.

"You're selling all of this?" asked Titus Jones.

"Yes. The old man died owing me rent," Professor Carswell said. "He sometimes got money from Europe, so I wrote to that address, but I've had no answer. No one has come, and I need the money."

While Uncle Titus and the Professor discussed price, Jupiter looked at the meager possessions of Joshua Cameron with disappointment. There was nothing at all that looked really valuable.

"What happened to Mr. Cameron, Hal?" he asked.

"He just got sick," Hal Carswell said. "I tried to help him, but he was delirious with fever. Babbled about canvases and zigzags. The doctor came and wanted to move him to a hospital, but Mr. Cameron died first. He was just old and sick."

"Well," Pete said, "there sure isn't much in his stuff that a thief would want, Jupe. A mistake, I guess."

Jupiter nodded glumly. They loaded Joshua Cameron's things onto the salvage yard truck and started home along the winding canyon road. As the truck passed the mouth of the barranca, Jupiter frowned.

"Thieves don't usually pick a house by mistake," the stocky First Investigator said thoughtfully.

"I guess we'll never know for sure what that man wanted," Pete said.

"I suppose not," Jupiter said, and sighed.

But both boys were wrong.

A CLIENT ARRIVES

One afternoon a week later, Jupiter and the third member of The Three Investigators, Bob Andrews, were working in the salvage yard. It was Bob who first saw the long, yellow Mercedes drive into the yard and stop in front of the office.

A small, elegant man got out of the dazzling automobile. His gray hair seemed to shine in the late afternoon sun like silver. He wore a white summer suit with a blue silk vest. He carried a slim black cane, and something glittered in his hand. For a moment he stopped and looked toward the boys. Then he stalked abruptly into the junkyard office.

Both boys gaped after the elegant little man. Then Jupiter suddenly gulped.

"I forgot! *We're* supposed to be watching the office for Uncle Titus. Come on."

The boys hurried toward the office. Just as they reached the yellow Mercedes, the rear door opened and a tall lady with high blue-gray hair stepped out. She wore a white silk dress and a simple diamond brooch. She stared down at the boys with regal eyes.

"I wish to speak with a Mr. Titus Jones. Is he here?"

"My uncle left me in charge of the yard, ma'am," Jupiter told the queenly woman.

"Indeed? Can one so young assume charge?"

"I think so, ma'am," Jupiter said firmly.

"Good." The lady smiled. "I like confidence, young man."

"Besides," Bob added, grinning at her, "we don't get many customers after five o'clock, anyway."

The lady laughed. "I like honesty, too. And you do have a customer now. My estate manager, Mr. Marechal, is already in your office. I suggest we join him."

As the boys followed the elegant lady into the office, the small, silver-haired man stepped quickly away from Uncle Titus's desk. Jupiter noticed that the record book of purchases made for the junkyard was on the desk, and seemed to have been moved.

"Armand," the imperious lady said, "it seems that these boys are in charge here."

"So?" The man bowed to the boys. They saw what had glittered in his hand outside — his cane had a large silver head. "Then I shall state our business. The Countess wishes to retrieve the possessions of the late Mr. Joshua Cameron sold to you by Professor Carswell. We will, of course, pay a suitable price to reimburse you for your trouble."

"Is there something valuable among them, sir?" Jupiter asked eagerly.

"They have only sentimental value, I fear," the tall lady said.

"The Countess is Joshua Cameron's sister," the man added.

Bob exclaimed, "Are you really a countess?"

"My late husband was a count, yes," said the Countess with a smile, "but my maiden name is Cameron. I am poor Joshua's younger sister. Joshua was eccentric, and a recluse, and since I am twenty years younger, we were not very close. Still, it grieves me that he died alone in a strange place."

"You see, boys," Mr. Marechal said, "we were in Africa until a few days ago, and only just received Professor Carswell's letter telling of Joshua's tragic death. We caught the first jet to America, but, alas, Professor Carswell had already sold Joshua's things to you for back rent. A paltry sum we will gladly double to have the possessions returned to us."

"We'll get them," Bob declared. "You just wait, Countess."

The boys took the purchase book and went out into the junkyard. Jupiter looked for the suitcases, the clothes, and the silver. Bob tried to locate the stuffed owl, the statue of Venus, and the binoculars. They both asked Hans and Konrad, the Bavarian brothers who worked in the yard, about the twenty paintings. Fifteen minutes later, the boys returned to the office dejected.

"I'm sorry," Jupiter said sadly. "We seem to have sold everything except the clothes."

"The clothes you may keep," Mr. Marechal said. "But you found nothing else? Not even his paintings?"

"That is peculiar," Jupiter acknowledged. "We don't sell many paintings, but they're all gone."

"Where?" Mr. Marechal asked.

Jupiter shook his head. "We keep a record of what we buy, Mr. Marechal, and from whom, but we don't keep a record of our customers. So many people come here and buy just one thing, and we all sell. Konrad, one of our helpers, thinks he sold all the paintings to one man, but he can't remember who. I don't think any of us will remember the customers."

"This is very unfortunate, boys," the Countess said.

"Can't you locate the things somehow?" Mr. Marechal said.

Jupiter's eyes brightened. "Well, sir, perhaps we could look for them, if . . ."

Jupiter hesitated. The Countess frowned.

"If what, young man," she said. "Come, speak up."

Jupiter drew himself up to seem as imposing as he could. "If you wish to hire us. It happens that Bob and I, with our friend, Pete, are investigators. Here are our cards."

The stout leader of The Three Investigators presented their business card, and their green card that stated:

This certifies that the bearer is a Volunteer Junior Assistant Deputy cooperating with the police force of

Rocky Beach. Any assistance given
him will be appreciated.

> (*Signed*) *Samuel Reynolds*
> *Chief of Police*

The Countess smiled. "Quite impressive, boys, but — "

"My pardon, Countess," Mr. Marechal interrupted, and nodded to the boys. "We are strangers here. The boys know the area, are experienced, and know what to look for. Besides, people might be more willing to return Joshua's things to boys. They appear quite intelligent. Why not let them try?"

The Countess considered. "Very well, Armand, perhaps you are right. I *would* like to have our family heirlooms and poor Joshua's last paintings."

"We'll find the things, ma'am," both boys said at once.

"Good," Mr. Marechal said. "We can be reached at The Cliff House Motel up the coast. We will be there a week. After that, the Countess must return to Europe. Good luck, boys."

The Countess and Mr. Marechal went to their Mercedes and drove off. As soon as the yellow car had gone, Bob exclaimed:

"Jupe, how do we — "

The Records and Research man of the trio stopped in mid-sentence. Jupiter was staring at a small blue coupe that drove past the driveway opening in the salvage yard fence and vanished down the street after the yellow Mercedes.

"That's curious," said Jupiter.

"What is?" asked Bob.

"That blue car started up just after the Mercedes left. It must have been parked out on the street."

"So?"

"Few people park there unless they are coming here — and we haven't had any customers in the last half hour except the Countess and Mr. Marechal."

"You think that blue car is following — "

Before Bob could finish, a boy on a bicycle rode into the junkyard. It was the slim, dark-haired son of Professor Carswell.

"Guys!" Hal Carswell cried as he saw them. "Has the Countess been here?"

"She just left, Hal," Bob said.

"Did you give her back Mr. Cameron's possessions?"

"We've sold most of them," said Jupe. "But I think we can get them back."

"Whew!" said Hal. "That's a relief! The Countess and Mr. Marechal came to our house early this afternoon. When Dad told them we'd sold Mr. Cameron's things to you, the Countess got real angry and said we should have waited for an answer to our letter. Mr. Marechal calmed her down and said we couldn't have known old Joshua had a sister. But I know Dad's worried. Maybe we shouldn't have sold the things. The Countess could make trouble if she doesn't get them back!"

"Tell me, Hal," said Jupe. "When the Countess and Mr. Marechal were at your house, did you happen to notice a blue coupe anywhere near?"

"A blue coupe . . . ?" Hal thought a minute. "Yes! There was one! A blue car went out the canyon road right after the Countess left. I remember noticing it because it was unfamiliar. We don't get much traffic on the road — it's a dead end and usually only the neighbors drive by. But what's this all about?"

"We just saw a blue car follow the Countess away from here, too!" said Bob.

"You mean someone is spying on her?"

"Apparently so," said Jupiter. He looked thoughtful. "First an intruder breaks into your cottage, Hal. Now someone is watching the Countess and Mr. Marechal. In both cases, old Joshua Cameron's possessions are involved. There's something mysterious about it all, fellows."

"Do you think old Joshua did have something valuable?" Bob asked.

"I don't know yet, Records. First we have to worry about getting back old Joshua's things from whoever bought them."

"Whoever bought them?" repeated Hal. "Don't you know who bought them?"

"We have no idea," Jupiter said blandly.

"Then," Hal said, startled, "how can you ever find them?"

Bob said, "I think I know."

"Yes," Jupiter said. "We'll use a Ghost-to-Ghost Hookup!"

JUPITER'S MISTAKE

"Ghost-to-Ghost?" Hal said. "But there aren't any ghosts!"

"Some scientists are no longer sure of that," Jupiter said. "But, actually, ghosts have nothing to do with our hookup system."

"Adults just think it's ghosts at work," Bob added, laughing.

Moments later, Uncle Titus drove into the junkyard, and Jupe and Bob were off duty until after dinner. With Hal, they slipped off to the secret headquarters of The Three Investigators — an old, damaged house trailer now hidden by piles of junk at one side of the salvage yard. The main entrance to it was

Tunnel Two, a large corrugated pipe that led under the surrounding junk to a trap door in the trailer's floor. Crawling through the pipe, the boys surfaced into a little room crowded with equipment — a desk, chairs, file cabinets, a private phone, and various devices that Jupiter had invented for the Investigators' work. Opening off the office room were a small lab and a darkroom.

Hal admired the setup, but quickly returned to the problem at hand. "How," he demanded again, "can you find Mr. Cameron's things if you don't even know who bought them?"

"How many friends do you have, Hal?" Jupiter asked.

"What? Gosh, maybe five good ones. Why?"

Jupiter explained that Hal would call his friends and give each a list of the items that were wanted. Each friend would call five other friends, who in turn would call five more, and so on. Jupiter, Bob, and Pete would do the same.

"In a few hours, every kid in Rocky Beach will be looking for the things. Maybe kids as far as Los Angeles or Oxnard."

"Wow!" Hal said. He mentally added up the thousands of people who could be reached. "You could contact the whole world!"

"Well," Jupiter said, "we haven't tried the world, but if we could solve the language problem, it would probably work."

"How soon will it get results?" Hal asked. "I have to go home for dinner, and Dad is taking me to Los Angeles tonight."

"Not before morning," Jupiter decided. "The kids we call can start looking after dinner when most people are at home. Our message will list the items we want, what we'll pay, and where to bring them. We'll also specify that the kids should call us first and describe what they've found. That way we can screen out the things that obviously weren't Mr. Cameron's, and we won't be flooded by kids coming here."

"We'll have to offer a reward," reminded Bob.

"Hmmm," mused Jupe. "Let's say that anyone who brings in a correct item will have his choice of anything in the junkyard priced at one dollar or less. And, of course, we'll pay back the purchase price of old Joshua's things."

They composed the message listing the items, and Jupiter called Pete to tell him what they were doing. Then the three boys went home for dinner. By eight o'clock that evening, every boy and girl in Rocky Beach was out looking for Joshua Cameron's belongings.

By nine the next morning, The Three Investigators were gathered in Headquarters waiting for results of the Ghost-to-Ghost Hookup. They watched the telephone expectantly.

"There will be a lot of wrong items," Jupiter pointed out, "but by having the kids telephone, we'll not waste their time."

Jupiter prided himself on his planning and foresight, but by ten o'clock something seemed wrong. The telephone in Headquarters hadn't rung once! Jupiter's confidence had begun to fade, and Pete looked uncomfortable.

Jupiter bit his lip. "Someone should have called by now."

There was a sudden knocking at the trap door up from Tunnel Two. The boys looked at each other uneasily. Bob finally went and opened the trap door. Hal Carswell climbed up into the room.

"Gosh, guys, why are you in here?" the Professor's son said. "Kids are all over the junkyard outside looking for you!"

"Outside?" Jupiter quavered. "But we told them . . ."

"Er, Jupe," Pete said slowly. "I've been trying to remember. We told the kids to call here, but I don't remember giving them our phone number."

"Gosh," Bob echoed, "neither do I, Jupe!"

"Phone number?" Hal said.

Jupiter reddened as he looked at the message he had written down the night before to pass along the Ghost-to-Ghost Hookup.

"I . . . I guess I forgot to put it in," Jupiter said. "I guess we better go out."

"Is Uncle Titus out there?" Pete asked Hal Carswell.

"I only saw those two big helpers of yours," Hal said. "They had kids all around them."

"I don't think I want to go out," Pete said.

Jupiter took a deep breath. "I'm afraid we have to."

They emerged into a scene of wild chaos.

"Oh no!" Pete groaned.

"Gee," Hal said, "they're still coming in!"

Jupiter only stared.

Boys and girls milled everywhere through the junkyard. They were shouting and running, and some climbed high on the mounds of junk. There were hundreds of them, like ants. They swarmed around Hans and Konrad, holding up the objects they had found

for the Ghost-to-Ghost. More rode in on bi-
cycles, in wagons, on scooters, and on foot.
There were even teen-agers on motorcycles
and in wildly painted cars.

"I do not know what you want!" Hans was
shouting.

"We did not ask for you to come!" Konrad
was protesting.

Suddenly, some of the kids saw Jupiter and
the boys.

"There! That must be them!" one boy
shouted.

In a second, the whole horde of kids poured
toward The Three Investigators and Hal.
Jupiter turned pale. He had once been a child
movie star named Baby Fatso, and ever since
fans had mobbed him in his acting days, Jupe
had hated crowds.

Bob cried, "What do we do, Jupe?"

"I . . . I . . ." Jupiter stammered.

"We run for it!" Pete yelled.

Suddenly, Hal Carswell stood up on a gaso-
line drum. Above the onrushing stampede of
kids, Hal shouted a stream of some strange
language and waved his arms commandingly.
Confused and stunned, the mob of kids hesitated and stared at him.

"Quick, Jupe," Pete urged, "what can we
give them *all* for a small reward. Hurry!"

"Give . . . I . . ." Jupiter stuttered. "Well . . . there's a barrel of old political campaign buttons. Maybe they . . ."

"Swell," Pete said. "Hold your hats!"

Pete strode out to the wild mob of kids, each with some item to sell to the boys.

"All right!" Pete shouted. "A valuable old political button for everyone! No one else will have the same ones! If you want one, form in five lines facing us! First line on the left for suitcases! Next line for stuffed owls and statues. Third line for binoculars. Fourth line for silver knives and forks. Last line for paintings! No pushing, everyone gets a turn. One of us will stand at the head of each line and inspect what you've brought. Okay, now form the lines!"

The kids, even the teen-agers, hurried to form the lines. They realized it was the quickest way to end the chaos.

"Good work, Second," Jupiter said approvingly to Pete.

"Thank Hal, he stopped them," Pete said. "One of us will have to examine two lines, and Hans better give out the buttons."

At each line, one of the boys quickly inspected each item as the kids filed past. Each person with a wrong item was sent to Hans for his political button for trying. After an hour the junkyard was almost empty again — and the boys had the stuffed owl, both suitcases, the binoculars, and the silverware.

"A girl gave me the address of where the statue of Venus is," Bob said, "but the lady who has it wouldn't sell it back. I gave the girl her full reward anyway."

"Good," Jupiter said. "You go and see if you can get the statue, Records. And Pete, you call Mr. Marechal and the Countess at The Cliff House Motel and tell them what we have."

The two Investigators hurried off.

"Gosh, it worked great, Jupiter," Hal Carswell said as he looked at what they had recovered. "Except, we didn't get any of the paintings!"

"I'm afraid someone from out of town may have — " Jupiter began, and stopped. He stared at a shiny car that had just come into the junkyard.

A tall, skinny youth not much older than the trio of investigators got out of the car. He was scowling nastily at Jupiter, and he was carrying a painting!

TROUBLE FROM AN
OLD ENEMY

"Would this be one of the paintings you want, Jones?" the skinny boy said.

"Skinny Norris!" Jupiter exclaimed. "What are you doing here?"

E. Skinner Norris glared at Jupiter. The nasty youth hated the trio of investigators, and out of jealousy had been trying to wreck anything they did ever since he first met them. Although not much older than they were, Skinny had a driver's license, because his father was a legal resident of another state. It made him feel superior to The Three Investigators.

"Never you mind," Skinny said. "Just tell

me if this is one of the paintings you're after."

Jupiter and Hal both recognized the painting as one of old Joshua Cameron's last works. Hal was about to say something when Jupiter spoke quickly:

"Well, I'm not exactly sure, Skinny. Where did you get it?"

"That's my business," Skinny snarled.

"We have to know you can sell it," Hal pointed out.

Skinny paled. "What do you mean by that?"

"I know *you* didn't buy it from us," Jupiter said.

"Maybe you stole it!" Hal declared.

"I did not!" Skinny said hotly, and then his eyes narrowed. "So, it *is* one of the right paintings! I thought it was."

"Yes," Jupiter admitted. "We'll buy it, Skinny."

"No, I don't think I'll sell it now," Skinny said, and went quickly back to his car.

Before the boys could stop him, Skinny had driven out of the junkyard.

Pete ran up from the office. "What was Skinny doing here?"

"He had one of Joshua's paintings!" Hal said.

"But he suddenly wouldn't sell it," Jupiter added.

"Gosh," Pete said, "and Mr. Marechal is coming over now."

While the boys waited for Mr. Marechal, Bob returned from trying to buy the statue of Venus.

"The lady still won't sell the statue," Bob reported.

That, and the loss of the painting, curbed their elation over the success of the Ghost-to-Ghost Hookup. But when Mr. Marechal arrived to claim the five items they had found, he was beaming.

"You are fine detectives, boys! I congratulate you."

"But we didn't get the statue," Bob said. "A Mrs. Leary, at 22 Rojas Street, has it, and she won't sell it back."

Jupiter explained what had happened with Skinny and the one painting they had found.

"Well, I have the address. I shall speak with Mrs. Leary myself," Mr. Marechal said. "As for this Norris boy, he lives here in Rocky Beach? A well-known family, you say?"

"Yes, sir," Pete said. "They've got a big house on the beach."

"Then I am sure you boys will find a way

to secure that painting, eh? Even one of Joshua's last works would please the Countess," Mr. Marechal said. "Now I shall pay you a three-dollar reward for each item, plus the purchase prices. That makes fifteen dollars for your services. Is that satisfactory?"

"Yes, sir!" all three Investigators said at once.

"Good." Mr. Marechal smiled. "And I shall await your equal success on the paintings, boys."

Jupiter wrote out a receipt for Mr. Marechal while the other boys put the retrieved possessions in the back of the Mercedes. With a small bow, Mr. Marechal returned to his car swinging his silverheaded cane, and Hal went home to report the morning's success to his dad.

After lunch, The Three Investigators met again in Headquarters. Jupiter sat at the desk looking thoughtful.

"Fellows," the First Investigator said, "I do not think Skinny ever intended to sell us that painting, at least not yet. I think he simply wanted us to identify it for him."

"Why, Jupe?" Bob asked.

"I'm not sure, Records. Possibly because he does know where the others are, and he wanted to be sure they were all genuine before he brought them to sell to us. Or possibly he is working for someone else who isn't sure just what old Joshua's paintings looked like. Perhaps whoever is in that blue coupe."

"Who could it be in that blue car?" Pete wondered.

"I don't know, Second," Jupiter admitted. "But we must try to find those twenty paintings for Mr. Marechal, and the way to do it is through Skinny."

"Maybe he just wants more money," Bob suggested.

"That's Skinny," Pete agreed. "Let's try calling him."

Jupiter did as Pete suggested, and switched on the loudspeaker attachment he had built for the telephone. Moments later, Skinny Norris's voice filled the room. "Stop pestering me, Fatso. I've got to go to my new job."

"Skinny, we'll pay twice what we sold the painting for," Jupiter said into his desk unit.

"What painting?" Skinny asked, and snickered.

"Why," Pete exploded, "you know what painting, Skinny!"

"You dumbbells must be dreaming," Skinny said.

There was a click, and the buzz of the dial

tone. Skinny had hung up. The Three Investigators stared at each other.

"We can watch him, First," Pete said. "Shadow him."

Jupiter sighed. "He has a car, Second. We only have bikes. Uncle Titus would let Hans or Konrad drive us in the small truck if we knew where to go, but we don't. We don't have any idea where Skinny got that painting."

"We can use our homing device on his car!" Bob said. "He said he had a job — maybe he got the painting there. His parents wouldn't let him work too far away. We could spread out on our bikes around his house, and maybe one of us could stay close enough to follow the homing signal to where he goes!"

"Well," Jupiter considered, "I guess it's certainly worth a try. We'll try to talk to him once more at his house and if that doesn't work, we'll use the . . ."

The distant sound of a voice made Jupiter stop speaking. Someone was calling his name. Pete went to the See-All. This was a crude but efficient periscope Jupiter had built to allow the boys to see out into the junkyard. Pete peered into the eyepiece.

"It's your Aunt Mathilda," Pete stated. "And she's got a man with her. She looks pretty mad!"

"What man, Second?" Jupiter asked.

"I never saw him before. Kind of short and heavy, in a dark suit and hat, and — Jupe! He's carrying a big, flat case!"

Jupiter looked into the See-All. "It's the kind of case you carry paintings in! Come on, fellows."

They hurried out through Tunnel Two.

THE LIMPING MAN

"Well, there you are!" Aunt Mathilda said as the boys appeared from behind piles of junk. "Where do you rascals get to out in that junk? No one can ever find you when we want you!"

"I'm sorry, Aunt Mathilda," Jupiter said.

"Don't sweet-talk me, Jupiter Jones," his aunt said briskly. "This is Mr. De Groot. Says he's an art dealer from Holland. He wants to ask you about those twenty paintings your Uncle and you bought out in Remuda Canyon last week. Though what anyone wants with twenty paintings of the same house, I don't know."

"It is not the subject that matters, madame," the short, heavy stranger said in a rough voice. "It is the skill."

"All I know is what I like," Aunt Mathilda said, "and I didn't like those paintings. Every one was different, but not one looked like a real house to me."

Aunt Mathilda stalked off to the office, leaving the boys with Mr. De Groot. The art dealer had fierce, dark eyes.

"I come from Amsterdam to meet Joshua Cameron," De Groot said bluntly. "I find he is dead. Then I hear from boys at my motel that a Three Investigators wish to locate twenty of his paintings! I learn that The Three Investigators are at The Jones Salvage Yard. Now I am here to buy those twenty paintings. You have them?"

Pete shook his head. "None of them were brought back, sir."

"None?" De Groot angrily paced a few steps in the yard, and glared at the boys. "I will pay well for them."

"Skinny Norris brought one painting, Mr. De Groot," Bob said, "but . . ."

Jupiter stared at the short, heavy Dutchman, and beyond him toward the entrance to the junkyard. As Bob started to explain about Skinny, Jupiter broke in:

"But it was the wrong painting, Mr. De Groot."

"It was not a Joshua Cameron?"

"I'm afraid it wasn't, sir," Jupiter said sadly.

Bob and Pete blinked at Jupiter, but they didn't say anything. They had learned not to question what their stout leader did, no matter how sudden or strange. De Groot stared at them, and scowled at Jupiter.

"I hope you are not lying to me," he said.

"I do not lie, sir," Jupiter said loftily.

"No, perhaps not," De Groot said, but his voice was suspicious. "This Norris you speak of, he is a tall, thin boy?"

"How did you know that?" Pete exclaimed.

"I have ways," De Groot snapped. "Is his family wealthy? Do they have an art collection? Are they buyers of art?"

"I think they have a small art collection," Bob acknowledged.

Jupiter's voice was innocent. "We really don't know Skinny Norris very well, sir. Not even where he lives, I'm afraid."

"Then you cannot help me?" De Groot watched them all.

"I wish we could, sir," Jupiter said.

"Yes," De Groot said, still watching them. "Then in case the paintings are returned here, you will call me at The Dunes Motel, yes? Remember, I will pay you well."

The boys nodded, and De Groot turned and walked off toward the entrance gate of the junkyard. Bob and Pete both stared after the art dealer. De Groot had a slight limp!

"Jupe!" Bob cried. "He has a — "

"Yes, Records, he has a limp," said Jupe. "That was the first thing I noticed when he began to pace a few minutes ago. As if he hurt his leg recently, fellows. Maybe from a fall into a barranca!"

"He could be that intruder we chased a week ago!" Bob said.

"That's why you didn't want to tell him about Skinny," Pete said, "and that Skinny's painting was old Joshua Cameron's."

"That was one reason, yes," Jupiter agreed.

Bob asked, "What was another reason, First?"

"I saw his car outside the yard," Jupiter said. "Look."

Outside the junkyard the art dealer was getting into a small, blue coupe! As they watched, he drove away.

"It's the car that's been following the Countess!" Pete cried.

"And I told him about Skinny and the painting," Bob groaned.

"You didn't tell him much," Jupiter said consolingly, "and I don't think what you said mattered. I think Mr. De Groot knew something about Skinny before he came here, and I think we had better get to Skinny again pretty fast!"

"Let's go!" Pete said.

"I can't go now, fellows," said Bob. "I've got to run an errand for my mother."

Jupiter thought. "All right, Bob, we'll go on ahead with the homing transmitter, and you can bring the receiver later if your errand won't take long."

"It won't!" Bob said.

"Good. Then we'll meet at Skinny's house."

Skinny Norris's house was a big redwood house on a small street of beach houses. It was right on the beach. An alley ran between the houses directly across the street from it. The whole street was thick with palms and hibiscus bushes.

Pete and Jupiter stopped their bikes behind a big hibiscus, across the street and down a ways from the Norris house. From there they could see the front and side entrances to the house, and the only entrance to the garage. Skinny's sports car was parked there.

"We'll talk to him first," Jupiter decided.

They walked their bikes up the path to the front door. A window on the second floor opened, and Skinny leaned out.

"What do you so-called detectives want now?"

"We just want to buy that painting, Skinny," Pete called up.

Skinny laughed. "Go fly a kite, Crenshaw!"

"We know you have the painting, Skinny," Jupiter said.

"Yah-yah! You don't know anything. Get out of here before I call the police on you for trespassing!"

Looking dejected, Pete and Jupiter rode their bikes away until they were out of sight of the house. Then they walked the bikes back to the thick hibiscus, where they crouched, hidden.

"I'll sneak up on Skinny's car from the beach and plant the homer on it," Jupiter said. "You watch the front and side doors of the house, and the garage, Pete. If Skinny comes out, whistle a warning."

"Okay," Pete agreed, "and I'll watch for Bob."

Jupiter turned to slip away toward the beach. The stout First Investigator suddenly stopped.

"Someone's near Skinny's house!" he whispered urgently.

Pete looked. A man in a uniform was turning into the narrow walk on the far side of Skinny's house. His cap was low on his forehead, shading his eyes. He walked awkwardly, as if thrown off balance by the heavy tool kit he carried.

"It's just a telephone man," Pete said, taking a breath.

Jupiter watched the telephone man disappear behind Skinny's house. He frowned. "Yes, I guess so. Only . . ."

"Only what, First?" Pete said.

"I don't know," Jupiter said slowly, and looked down the quiet, empty street. "Something's odd, but I can't put my finger on it."

"I'll keep my eyes open," Pete promised.

Jupiter nodded, and slipped away toward the beach. Pete settled behind the hibiscus to watch Skinny's house.

A small creek came down to the beach between Skinny's house and the next house. Dry now in summer, it was a good place for Jupiter to hide, and sneak up close to the garage without being seen.

Skinny was nowhere in sight. Jupiter checked the tiny homer transmitter, which contained a magnet that would hold the device on Skinny's car. Jupiter had made the instrument himself in his workshop. The transmitter sent out a tiny *beep-beep* signal that got louder and faster as you got nearer to it. The receiving instrument picked up the signal and also showed, by an arrow on a dial, the direction the signal came from.

All the boys had to do was plant the transmitter on a car, and with their receiver they could follow the car from far enough away to remain unseen.

Jupiter started to creep along the creek bed, and stopped. He saw that the telephone repairman had circled Skinny's house and was now on the garage side. He was bent over, working on the wires where they entered the house. Suddenly Jupiter realized what had seemed odd to him about the telephone man — there had been no telephone truck out on the street!

Whoever heard of a telephone man without his truck? The repairman was an imposter! Yet he *was* working on the telephone wires. Maybe tapping Skinny's phone? Forgetting about putting the homer on Skinny's car, Jupiter began to crawl along the dry creek bed to a spot where he could spy on the fake telephone man.

It was hard work for the overweight boy. He was puffing when he reached the place that he judged was right behind the "telephone man." When his panting had subsided, he raised his head carefully above the creek bank.

"Ulllppp!"

Jupiter found himself looking straight into the face of the fake telephone man. Only a foot away, the dark eyes glared at Jupiter — the eyes of the Dutch art dealer, De Groot!

The Dutchman held a wicked-looking knife, and glared menacingly.

Pete, crouched behind the hibiscus, had seen no sign of Skinny or of Jupiter. Bob still hadn't arrived with the homer receiving instrument.

"Pete!"

The voice came from behind the house directly across the street from Pete, from the direction of the beach.

"Pete! Help!"

Pete ran across the quiet street and turned behind the house. A hand clamped over his mouth. Another hand twisted his arm. Pete was captured!

PRISONERS!

Bob saw the two bikes as he rode up toward Skinny's house. Pete and Jupiter's bikes behind a hibiscus! But where were the two investigators? In dismay, Bob looked up and down the empty street.

As he brought his bike abruptly to a halt, he heard a car start in the alley across from Skinny's house. A blue coupe came tearing out of the alley, turned right with a squeal of tires, and raced away along the street.

Bob stared after the blue coupe. The art dealer's car! What had De Groot been doing?

Beep-beep-beep-beep!

Bob heard the sudden beeping from his

pocket. He pulled out the homing receiver. The arrow was pointing right up the street, and the beeps were loud and rapid — but slowing and diminishing. Bob guessed at once what had happened.

Jupiter and Pete had not placed the homer on Skinny's car. They had it with them! And they were in the blue coupe of the art dealer, De Groot!

Frantically Bob rode his bike after the blue coupe, which was already out of sight. He followed the beeps of the homer, and reached the main coastal frontage road. He pursued the beeps left toward the northern outskirts of Rocky Beach. Twice he lost the beeps when the blue coupe pulled too far away, and twice he picked up the beeps again as the coupe was forced to stop for something like a traffic light.

Bob stopped for nothing, not even for the traffic lights. But the third time he lost the beeps, they did not start again.

In despair, Bob pedaled on, searching the main road along the coast, looking up and down the empty side streets as Rocky Beach thinned into open country.

Bound with telephone cord and gagged, Pete and Jupiter lay squeezed into the trunk of De Groot's blue coupe. Just before the car had left the alley across from Skinny's house, Jupiter had managed to turn on the homer. Both boys thought they had heard the squeak of bicycle brakes out on the street. But now some ten minutes had passed, and the blue coupe had stopped or slowed only twice.

There was no way that Bob could follow them now, even if he did know that De Groot had captured them.

Mentally, Jupiter kicked himself for not recognizing that the repairman's awkward gait was actually De Groot's limp.

Another ten minutes, no more, and the blue coupe turned off the road and parked. The trunk was flung open. De Groot pulled the boys out one at a time and hurried them into the last unit in a small motel. The dark-eyed art dealer had not said a single word since he had caught Jupiter.

Inside the motel room, De Groot sat the boys side by side on a couch, ungagged them, took out his evil-looking knife, and sat facing them. His deep eyes glittered angrily.

"So! This Skinny Norris did not bring to you the right painting. You were not interested in his painting. You did not even know where he lived, eh? Liars! You want to steal old Joshua's paintings for yourselves!"

"We do not!" Pete said hotly. "We're finding them for the Countess. They belong to her!"

"Ah, that is it, eh? You are working with the Countess and Armand Marechal. What have they told you?"

"That they want to recover the Countess's family heirlooms," Jupiter said. "We've found everything except the paintings."

"You lie again. You must know more. What are Marechal's plans? What are they actually looking for? What message did Joshua Cameron send them?"

"What we know," Pete said, "is that you've been following the Countess everywhere, and you were at Professor Carswell's house over a week ago trying to — "

Jupiter broke in quickly. "Why do you think Joshua Cameron sent a message to the Countess? She wasn't close to — "

"Do not try to fool me, boy!" De Groot snapped, and he looked at Pete. "You were about to say that you know I was at Carswell's house?"

Pete swallowed. The Second Investigator realized that Jupiter didn't want De Groot to know that they suspected him of being the mysterious intruder a week ago at Remuda Canyon.

"Uhhh, we know you were at Professor Carswell's house the first day the Countess and Mr. Marechal arrived," Pete said, a little lamely.

De Groot studied the boys fiercely. "No. Someone was at Carswell's before the Countess arrived. Someone mysterious, eh? And you two think it was me. Why?"

The boys were silent.

"So? You will not reveal what made you suspect me? And you do not know of any message sent by old Joshua? You have talked with Professor Carswell and his son. Perhaps old Joshua gave them a spoken message, eh? Some last words?"

"We don't know of any, sir," Jupiter said politely.

The art dealer studied them. "Bah! I think you are stupid boys who do not know what you are doing!"

He glared at the boys, and stood up. "But perhaps you know too much, eh?"

De Groot held his long knife and watched the boys malevolently.

Bob rode his bike onward along the coast road in an agony of indecision. Alone, what chance did he have of finding the blue coupe?

But if he stopped to call Chief Reynolds, he could lose any trail his friends tried to leave.

So he rode on as fast as he could. The road north of town was now lined with motels. He listened for the beep of the homer, and looked for the blue car.

De Groot had been limping around the room, holding his wicked knife, for some ten minutes. He did not seem to be able to make up his mind.

"What must I do with you, eh? You are a nuisance, confound it! You are in my way, bah!"

Jupiter gulped. "Is there something valuable in Joshua Cameron's . . . ?"

"You are annoying me!" De Groot growled. "What would you say to working for me instead of the Countess?"

"We already have a client," Jupiter said stiffly.

"Foolish boy! Well, I cannot let you — "

The ringing of the telephone made the art dealer whirl. He stared at the instrument as if it were a snake. Then, watching the boys, he backed to the phone and picked up the receiver.

"Yes?" he said, and his eyes suddenly

lighted. "What? A boy? . . . Norris? . . . Yes, I know him. . . . No, do not send him here, I will come to the office. Hold him there!"

As De Groot hung up, his grin was triumphant. "It seems I must postpone tending to you two. The boy you hardly know, Master Norris, is here to see me!"

Pete groaned. "I knew Skinny was up to something!"

"You can't trust Skinny Norris, Mr. De Groot," Jupiter said.

"I trust no one, boy," De Groot snapped.

He gagged the boys again, and left the unit the back way. Pete and Jupiter struggled in their bonds, but it was no use. They sank back on the couch — just as the back door opened again! Helpless, the boys stared at the opening door.

Bob stood there grinning at them.

Then the smallest of the trio hurried to them, untied their bonds, and removed the gags.

"Boy!" Pete exclaimed. "Are we glad to see you. How did . . . ?"

"I followed the homer, but then I lost it. I just kept on riding. I'd almost given up when I picked up the signal again. I still didn't know where you were — until I remembered the name of De Groot's motel: The Dunes."

"Good work, Records," Jupiter said. "Now let's go!"

"But what about Skinny?" Pete objected. "He's in the motel office right now, probably selling De Groot the paintings."

Bob laughed. "Skinny isn't selling anything. He isn't even here. That was me on the telephone. De Groot is so eager, he didn't notice my voice wasn't the motel clerk's."

"But by now he knows," Jupiter said. "Out the front, quick!"

They hurried to the front door. The coast was clear. They ran across the motel grounds to Bob's bike.

"Pete can pedal," Jupiter decided. "He's the strongest. I'll ride the rear, and Bob can ride the handlebars. Hurry!"

They had pedaled less than twenty yards when they heard a cry of rage behind them. De Groot was in front of the room they had just left. He began to run after them, but he limped, and even on the overloaded bike they pulled away. De Groot turned and ran back toward the motel.

"He'll get his car!" Jupiter said. "We have to hide."

"No, we don't," Bob said, and held up a handful of colored wires. "I pulled the ignition wires from his car."

"Fine thinking, Records," Jupiter said admiringly. "However, he'll find another car soon. I suggest we pedal fast."

Pete puffed and groaned. "What do you mean — *we?*"

Minutes later, a man in a truck stopped to give them and the bike a lift into Rocky Beach. They retrieved the other two bikes, and rode home just in time for their dinners. Before they went to bed, they met once more in Headquarters.

Jupiter was serious. "There is something very strange about it all, men. De Groot seems to think there is something important that old Joshua Cameron would have left a message about. We must talk to the Countess and Mr. Marechal."

But there was no answer to their telephone call.

"We'll try again in the morning," Jupiter decided. "Meanwhile, I think we must learn more about Joshua Cameron. First thing tomorrow, Bob, you will research old Joshua at the library."

A SUDDEN SUSPICION

In the library the next morning, Bob hurried straight to the reference section. Most people weren't allowed in the reference stacks, but Bob worked part-time at the library. The librarian, Miss Bennett, only smiled at him as he walked by her. He found the art reference shelves — and stared. Almost all the big, heavy art volumes were gone!

Miss Bennett looked up as Bob came out from the stacks.

"Is something wrong, Robert?"

"Miss Bennett, where are all the art reference books?"

"A man has them all in the small reading room. He's been here since we opened, and yesterday, too. Do you want one in particular? I could ask him if he has finished with it."

"No, thank you," Bob said quickly. "I'll just look up something else until he's finished."

The moment he was out of Miss Bennett's sight, Bob hurried to the small reading room. He looked in cautiously. He saw the high stack of art books, and someone hidden behind them. As he watched, the person took another book off the stack, and Bob saw his face — Professor Carswell!

Bob ducked back quickly. His mind raced. Professor Carswell was studying all the art books! Excited, Bob made himself sit quietly where he could watch the door to the small reading room. He wondered if he should follow the Professor. But by the time Professor Carswell came out of the small room, Bob had decided that Jupiter would want him to do his research first. They could always locate the Professor.

So he checked out all the books Professor Carswell had returned, and settled down to research old Joshua Cameron.

* * *

Jupiter frowned. "Professor Carswell was studying the same books?"

"He sure was, First," Bob said. "All the art books!"

"Gosh," Pete said. "Why is he so interested in art?"

The three boys were in their hidden trailer in the junkyard. It was well after lunch, and Bob had just arrived with his report. Jupiter pondered the news of Professor Carswell and Bob's research.

"But you found absolutely nothing about Joshua Cameron in all those reference books?" Jupiter said slowly.

"Not a word," Bob said. "And two of the books list every artist in the world. At least, they say they do."

"It's possible he might be listed elsewhere," Jupiter decided. "But that would still make him very obscure."

"Then why would De Groot want his paintings so much?" Pete wondered.

"Maybe it's not the paintings he really wants," Bob suggested. "Maybe there's something else valuable that old Joshua had, and that the Countess and Mr. Marechal don't know about."

Jupiter nodded. "That would explain that mysterious intruder the first day. Perhaps he wanted to get whatever is valuable before anyone came to claim old Joshua's things. But the Professor sold them to Uncle Titus, and that intruder is still trying to find whatever it is."

"Just the way that De Groot is doing!" Pete said.

"Then what makes Professor Carswell so interested in art books all of a sudden?" Bob wanted to know.

Jupiter scratched his nose. "You recall that De Groot was interested in a message, any last words of old Joshua's. Perhaps there was a message. Hal said the old man was delirious, and babbling. Perhaps he was trying to give a message, and Professor Carswell knows something we don't."

"And something the Countess doesn't!" Bob said.

"I think," Jupiter said, "that we will take a ride out to Remuda Canyon."

Hal Carswell said, "Gosh, no, guys. I don't know why my Dad would study art books."

The four boys were on the shaded front lawn of the big house in Remuda Canyon.

"Did old Joshua talk much about his paintings?" Jupiter asked.

"Not much," Hal said. "He tried to teach

me to paint, but I can't even draw. I remember he did say something funny once. He said he was the most expensive painter in the world, but that no one knew it! He laughed when he said that. I don't know why."

"It sure doesn't make much sense," Pete declared.

"No, it certainly doesn't seem to," Jupiter agreed.

Hal said, "I don't understand what's going on, guys. Old Joshua lived here alone and no one ever came to see him. But now that he's dead, everyone is interested in him. The Countess and Mr. Marechal are inside the house now talking to Dad again."

"Gosh, maybe they've discovered something!" Pete said.

"Let's find out," Jupiter decided.

In the living room of the big, old house, Professor Carswell leaned on the mantelpiece facing Mr. Marechal and the Countess. The Countess smiled when she saw the boys.

"Ah, our young detectives. Still at work? You have indeed done well so far," the elegant lady said.

"We haven't found the paintings yet, ma'am," Jupiter said. "Didn't Joshua ever show or sell his work?"

"No, Jupiter, he was a simple amateur.

Still, I would like to have his last paintings. I hope you will continue searching, and find them."

"We will," Jupiter said, and added, "if someone else doesn't get them before we do."

"Someone else?" Mr. Marechal said, his voice puzzled.

"A man named De Groot, who calls himself an art dealer," Jupiter said. "He's been following you, and he wants Joshua's paintings."

The First Investigator related De Groot's actions, and told of the boys' narrow escape. The Countess was horrified.

"Why, that is terrible! You boys must be careful. I cannot understand such an interest in my brother. What could the man really want?"

"I don't know yet," Jupiter admitted, "but De Groot isn't the only one interested in paintings. Professor Carswell has been studying art books in the library."

Everyone looked at Professor Carswell. Hal watched his dad uneasily. Mr. Marechal glowered.

"Are you aware of something we are not, Carswell?" the silver-haired manager demanded.

"No, Marechal. I was simply as puzzled as

the Countess says she is," Professor Carswell said. "I wondered about all this sudden interest in old Joshua, so I went to the library to see if he was known elsewhere. But I found nothing. Which leaves me at a loss to explain the interest — or the mysterious intruder who came here earlier."

The Countess started. "There was an intruder here, Professor? You mean, *before* Mr. Marechal and I arrived? Someone who tried to steal some of Joshua's things, perhaps?"

"A week before you came, Countess," Bob explained, "and we don't really know what he wanted."

"I see," the Countess said, looking at Mr. Marechal.

"This De Groot, perhaps," Mr. Marechal said. "He seems to have some great interest in Joshua we don't understand."

"He sure does!" Pete agreed.

"Professor Carswell and Hal," Jupiter said, "De Groot seemed to think that old Joshua must have left some message for someone. You told us that Joshua was delirious and mumbling crazy words before he died. Could he have been trying to tell you something? Leave a message for someone?"

"It's quite possible, Jupiter. He was most insistent on trying to talk," the Professor said. "But I have no idea what he had on his mind. His words made no sense to me at all. Something about *zigzag* and *wrong* and *canvas*. He did say the word *paintings* a lot, and something about *masters*. Hal was with him more at the end than I was. Do you recall much, Hal?"

Hal nodded sadly. "I can't remember exactly, but he kept babbling words like: *Tell them, tell them . . . zig . . . zig when zag . . . wrong way . . . master . . . my paintings . . . my canvas . . . canvas . . . wrong to zigzag . . . tell 'em . . . wrong.* Over and over, sort of like that. The same words."

They all looked at each other as if one of them might know what old Joshua's ramblings meant. But none of them did. Even Jupiter looked blank.

"I can't make anything of that," Mr. Marechal said.

"No," the Countess sighed. "I'm afraid it was delirium."

"Professor?" Jupiter said. "Did Joshua keep all his possessions in the cottage?"

"I believe he did, Jupiter, yes."

The First Investigator nodded. "Well, we'd

better go. I still think Skinny Norris knows who has the paintings."

"Be careful, boys," the Countess said. "I'm quite worried about you. You will call us if there is any problem?"

The boys said they would. Outside, they got on their bikes and rode off. As they passed the mouth of the small barranca, out of sight of the house, Jupiter suddenly turned left into the gully. Startled, Pete and Bob followed.

"What are we doing, Jupe?" Bob asked, confused.

"I'm convinced that old Joshua *was* trying to leave some message with those babbling words," Jupiter declared. "I don't know what message yet. But the old man never left the cottage, so if he hid anything it should still be there. Follow me."

Leaving their bikes, they made their way along the barranca and into the cottage the back way. For a moment they stared around the silent cottage, trying to decide where to search first. All at once, they heard someone coming outside.

"Quick!" Jupiter whispered. "We'll hide and watch!"

They watched from the bedroom, and saw Hal Carswell come into the cottage. The boy hurried to a corner of the living room, lifted up a loose board, and reached down under the floor. The Investigators stepped out.

"So you know what old Joshua hid, Hal!" Jupiter accused.

The boy jumped up, startled, hiding something in his hand.

A BLACK HOLE

"Wow!" Hal gulped. "You fellows sure scared me."

"What did you take from under the floor!" Pete demanded.

"Take? Why, just this, guys." Hal showed them a large, old-fashioned key. He stared at them. "Hey, you came back to search the cottage! You think old Joshua hid something?"

"We consider that a possibility," Jupiter acknowledged.

"So do I!" Hal said eagerly. "After you left, I suddenly remembered something.

Dad's still talking to the Countess and Mr. Marechal, so I came over here alone."

"What did you remember, Hal?" Bob asked.

"That old Joshua used to store his paintings in the adobe back in the canyon. It's empty — my dad keeps it locked because it's historic and he doesn't want vandals damaging it. But I gave old Joshua the key when he first came here."

"And that's the key to the adobe?" Jupiter asked.

Hal nodded. "I figured that with Dad and the others talking, and you guys gone home, I'd search the adobe by myself."

"Maybe we'd all better go, then," Jupiter decided.

In the afternoon sun, Hal led the trio of investigators along the barranca away from the road. The gully wound past the Carswell house and then curved rather sharply back into the canyon. After a while Hal struck off to the left into the chaparral. The other boys followed, breaking through the thick, tangled growth until they reached a small clearing of hard-baked clay. In it was a low house with a wooden roof and shuttered windows. The old cabin, built of the local sun-dried clay brick called adobe, was silent and remote.

"It was built by the original Spanish owners of the canyon," Hal explained. "At least a hundred and fifty years ago. The only heat's a fireplace, and there's no bathroom."

Hal unlocked the door, which was made of thick hand-hewn planks, with wrought-iron bands and hinges. Inside, the boys saw that the adobe was almost completely empty. The wooden floor was thick with dust and dirt. Beyond the small main room, there was a smaller bedroom and a kitchen. The few windows were set in deep embrasures and shuttered from outside. A dim light filtered through the cracks in the shutters, and it was cool.

"Gosh," Pete said, "the walls must be three feet thick!"

"That's how they built with adobe," Jupiter informed them. "Adobe doesn't have the strength of regular brick, so it has to be built thick to carry the weight. Pete, you see what you can find in the kitchen, and Bob, you look in that bedroom. Hal and I will examine this main room."

Jupiter and Hal found unused canvases and cans of linseed oil and thinner, but no finished paintings. There was one ornate gold frame. Jupiter looked at the thick frame with a thoughtful expression.

"I wonder why old Joshua left this frame empty?" he asked.

"He had someone else's painting in it when he first came here," Hal said. "Just an imitation painting, you know? A print, he called it. He said he didn't like prints, and got rid of it."

"But not the frame," Jupiter pointed out. "Look at the design on the frame, Hal."

"Why, it's all zigzags! You think he was talking about this frame when he babbled about zigzags?"

"It's thick enough to hide something in."

The two boys examined the ornate frame, studying its joins and pressing on all the zigzag ridges. Jupiter shook his head.

"I can't see where anything could be hidden," the First Investigator said.

Pete came from the kitchen. "If there's anything hidden in that kitchen, it's in the walls."

"We can't see much out here, either," Hal said.

"Fellows!" Bob called from the bedroom. "In here!"

In the tiny bedroom, Bob stood over a battered old mattress that lay in a corner. Its cover had diagonal stripes.

71

"There's something inside this mattress," Bob said.

Pete felt the mattress where Bob indicated. "Gosh, there sure is! Like a bag full of stones. Maybe jewels!"

"Cut it open, Second," Jupiter said excitedly.

Pete took out his pocket knife and cut open the old mattress. The boys crowded around to look inside. They saw a cache of small, dark, almost round little objects like stones.

"What is it?" Hal said perplexed.

"Acorns and pine nuts," Jupiter said in chagrin. "It's the storehouse of a ground squirrel or field mouse."

The boys all stared at the little cache of nuts, and then they began to laugh. The difference between jewels and nuts was so great that it was hilarious. They laughed until the tears came down their faces.

They were laughing so hard that they didn't notice the bedroom door swinging closed until it shut tight with a heavy thud!

Pete stopped laughing and stared at the door. "What . . . ?"

There was a rasping sound as the bolt shot home outside, and they were locked into the bedroom.

"We're locked in!" Hal cried. "Hey! Hey out there!"

"Open the door! We're in here!" Bob shouted.

Pete began to pound on the heavy door. "Hey!"

"Wait!" Jupiter said.

The others stopped shouting and banging. Out in the main room someone was moving around. Whoever it was moved slowly, tapping the walls and floor, smashing the canvases and the one frame, banging linseed oil and thinner cans.

"It's a search," Jupiter whispered.

The noisy search went on a few more minutes. Then all was silent. The outside door closed, and the boys heard it lock.

"Oh, no," groaned Hal. "I left the key in the lock!"

They began to yell and pound on the walls again.

It was dark outside. Faint beams of moonlight came through the cracks in the heavy shutter on the single bedroom window.

Hours had passed. The boys had shouted themselves hoarse. The adobe was too far from the big house for them to be heard. The door and window were locked tight, and the walls were too thick to dig through with Pete's pocket knife. They had found a hollow spot under the floor where the basement was, but no way down. The boys sat on the old mattress, utterly discouraged.

"We're already late for dinner," Pete groaned.

"It looks to me like we're going to be late for a lot more than dinner," Bob said gloomily. "We're trapped in here good."

"We're going to be in trouble at home," Jupiter said with a sigh.

Hal said, "My dad'll miss me soon. He'll find us."

"You come back here a lot, Hal?" Pete asked.

"No," Hal said uneasily, "I guess not. Anyway, there's a lot of other places I'd go first."

"Then it could be a long wait for your dad," Bob said.

The boys all thought about that in silence. Pete got up and stamped on the floor next to a closet that was built out from one corner. The tall Second Investigator listened to the hollow sound.

"If only we could get down to the basement under here," Pete said. "There might be a way out. But all we've got is my pocket knife."

Hal got up and stamped along the wall beside Pete, listening again to the hollow sound. "I never knew there was a cellar under the adobe," he said. "I wonder why they built one. People don't have basements much in California."

"No, they don't," said Jupiter. "Especially not in an old adobe." He thought a moment and suddenly sat up excitedly. "Of course, of course! They didn't build cellars under these old adobes. But when the Americans and Spanish people were enemies, they often built escape tunnels! I think there's a passage under there!"

Jupiter studied the little room. "I would think there would be a way down to an escape passage from every room, but . . ." His eyes fixed on the closet door. "We didn't really examine that closet, fellows!"

Pete got to the closet first. It was a narrow closet with a heavy layer of dust and dirt on the floor. Bob and Pete brushed away the grime. Pete took out his pocket knife and probed in the cracks between the floor boards.

"This section moves!" Pete cried.

Bob and Pete lifted up a whole section of floor. Under it was dirt, and a trap door with a rusted iron ring in the center. Bob and Pete grabbed the ring, and the trap door swung up, revealing a narrow black hole. The boys stared down.

"Can anyone see the bottom?" Bob asked nervously.

"No," Hal said. "It's just all black."

"If you fellows think I'm jumping down a hole when I can't see the bottom," Pete declared, "you're crazy! I'll stay here."

"Whoever locked us in might come back," Jupiter said.

"Oh, no!" Pete moaned. "Okay — someone go first!"

"If only we hadn't left our flashlights on the bikes," Jupiter said.

The black hole gaped up at them.

It was Bob who finally stepped up to the hole.

"Well, here goes," the smallest boy said. "Geronimo, fellows!"

Bob lowered himself into the hole, held onto the edge for a moment — and dropped down into the blackness.

A CHASE IN THE NIGHT

Jupiter, Pete, and Hal peered down into the black hole.

"Bob?" Pete called.

A voice rose out of the blackness. "It's a dirt tunnel, all right, fellows. I can't see anything, but I can feel the walls. Wait a minute."

The three boys up in the closet heard movement below. It seemed hours, but it was only minutes before Bob spoke again.

"The tunnel only goes about six feet one way, back under the living room. There's another trap door at the end, but I can't budge it. Besides, our friend locked the front door, too. The other way, going away from the house, seems clear."

Pete was uneasy. "How do we know where it goes, Jupe?"

"We could get lost," Hal said.

Jupiter bit his lip. He called down, "Bob? How is the air down there? Can you feel any movement of air?"

"No movement," Bob said, "but the air seems fresh, all right."

Up in the closet Jupiter hesitated. He looked down into the black hole. Where did it lead?

"This tunnel might be very dangerous," the leader of the Investigators said at last. "If it caves in, that's the end of The Three Investigators — and Hal. But we're not getting anywhere just sitting in this room. And I don't think we should risk waiting for the one who locked us in to come back. This time he might . . ."

"You just convinced me," Pete said hastily.

The Second Investigator lowered himself into the black hole, and dropped from sight. Hal went next, and finally Jupiter.

At the bottom of the narrow tunnel they all tried to see each other, but it was too dark in the passage. It was also cold. Each of the boys felt the others shivering.

"We better move," Pete said, taking charge. "I'll lead, Jupe comes second, then Hal, and Bob at the rear. Each of you hold onto the belt of the person in front, so we don't lose anyone. Okay, let's go."

They went slowly along the pitch black passage, Pete feeling his way at each step. The passage had a low ceiling, and they had to crouch as they inched along.

"It seems to be going straight," Pete announced after a time. "But I'm not sure. I've lost my sense of direction."

In complete darkness, the four boys moved cautiously on. Each time Pete took a step, it seemed harder to put his foot down. They spoke less and less, the dark and silence deep in the earth weighing them down.

"Pete," Jupiter said, "did I feel something moving?"

They all froze.

"Air?" Bob said. "Is the air moving, fellows?"

Pete moved ahead a little faster. There was a small turn in the passage — and they all saw it ahead. A patch of lighter darkness!

"It's an opening!" Pete cried.

Another twenty steps, and they stood out in the open night. For a few moments they just grinned at each other. They were safe —

out of the adobe, and out of the terrible blackness of the passage. The moonlight seemed as
bright as day after the tunnel.

"We're in the barranca," Hal said, looking
around.

The steep sides of the barranca reached
above them. When they looked back at the
mouth of the small tunnel, they saw that it
was completely hidden by an overhang of the
bank and a thick growth of manzanita in
front of it.

"Now," Jupiter announced, undaunted,
"we'll go back and . . ."

"Agghhhh!" A cry echoed through the
moonlight.

A sharp cry not ten yards away, ending
in a crash and a heavy thud!

"What the . . . ?" Pete quavered.

A form loomed up before them in the night.

"Who's there?" a rough voice said. "So!
You kids!"

The boys saw the fierce face of the so-
called art dealer, De Groot, like a ghost in the
moonlight. He limped toward them, his suit
covered with dust and debris as if he had
fallen into the barranca.

The boys ran.

"Stop, you . . . !"

They ran toward the far end of the barranca where they had left their bikes. Behind them, the art dealer pursued, stumbling in the rocky gully. They ran faster in the night.

"There are the bikes!" Pete cried.

Pete redoubled his speed — and ran full tilt into a man! Hands grabbed him but Pete broke away.

"Watch out!" Pete cried. "Run, guys!"

The man tried to intercept the other boys, who dodged around him.

"Hal! It's me!"

"Dad!"

Professor Carswell stood in the moonlight beside the boys' bikes.

"De Groot," Pete panted. "He's chasing us!"

"He locked us in the old adobe!" Hal exclaimed.

"We found a secret tunnel," Bob said, "or we'd still be there!"

The Professor peered back up the barranca. "I don't see anyone behind you now, boys."

The barranca was silent in the moonlight.

"He was there, sir," Jupiter said, and told about what had happened in the old adobe. "After he trapped us, he searched the adobe, too. He must have had the same idea we did."

"And someone just searched the cottage again," Professor Carswell said. "I expect it was this De Groot, too."

"Sure it was, Dad," Hal said. "Then he must have come back to get us, found us gone, and tried to catch us again. But he fell into the barranca, and we heard him in time to run."

"If I hadn't been looking for Hal, and found the bikes, you could all have been in serious danger," Professor Carswell said. "You didn't do anything wrong, I admit. But I don't like this De Groot being around. This could be getting too serious for boys!"

JUPITER MAKES
SOME DEDUCTIONS

When The Three Investigators returned home that evening, they all received scoldings for missing dinner. Aunt Mathilda muttered that the devil found work for idle hands, but she was fortunately distracted from assigning extra chores to Jupiter by the start of her favorite TV program. Pete was supposed to have mowed the lawn after dinner, and his father told him do it first thing in the morning. So when Pete finally scrambled up into Headquarters the next day, he found that he was the last to arrive.

"Had to mow the lawn, fellows," Pete started to explain.

He stopped. Jupiter and Bob sat slumped around the desk. Bob was totally dejected, and Jupiter looked ill.

"You look like someone died!" Pete said. "No, I don't mean that. With us, that could be true. But what's wrong, guys?"

"Mr. Marechal just fired us," Bob said sadly.

Jupiter sighed. "He called a few minutes ago. Professor Carswell told him what happened last night at the adobe. Mr. Marechal said that the situation was becoming too dangerous and the police should be called in. He didn't think we could do much more anyway. He's going to send a small bonus."

"Gosh," Pete said, dropping into a chair. "Our first failure!"

"With so much that is still confusing," Jupiter moaned.

"Well," Bob said glumly, "I guess we'll just have to stay confused."

Jupiter nodded slowly, but the stout leader of the trio said nothing for a time. His eyes seemed to be seeing something very far away. Pete watched him.

"Don't turn in your badge yet, Bob," said Pete. "I've got a hunch Jupiter isn't going to stay fired, or confused. But Mr. Marechal might get mad if we keep nosing around, Jupe."

"Then we must convince him to allow us to continue," Jupiter declared. "The Three Investigators do not leave a case until it is completed!"

"How do we convince him to let us go on?" Bob asked.

"By showing him that there is more to this affair than he realizes. A mystery, Records! And by proving to him that we are the ones to solve the puzzle!"

Pete shook his head. "I don't know, First. Maybe Mr. Marechal is right. We don't have much to go ahead on."

"But we do! We have Joshua Cameron's last words, and our deductions."

"What deductions?" Pete said.

Jupiter leaned across the desk. "First, that old Joshua must have had something more valuable, or at least important, than was suspected. Second, that possibly more than one person knows this. Third, that the missing twenty paintings are somehow part of the secret. And, fourth, that old Joshua's last delirious words were meant as a message!"

The round-faced leader of the team sat back. "Now all we have to do is solve the

riddle of Joshua Cameron's last words —
provided we've been told the true words."

"You think Hal and his dad are lying?"
Bob exclaimed.

"We know the Professor needs money,"
Jupiter said. "We know that Joshua didn't
pay his rent the last months, and the Professor actually advanced him money. The
Professor could have known there was something valuable all along, or he could have
guessed it when that intruder broke in that
first day."

"I don't think Hal would lie," Pete objected.

"Perhaps not," Jupiter said. "Then let us
assume that Joshua's last words are correct
as reported. I have written them down as Hal
and the Professor told them."

Jupiter took out a sheet of paper and put it
on the table.

"According to the Professor, Joshua used
the words *paintings, zigzag, wrong, canvas,*
and *masters,*" Jupiter read. "Hal, who was
with the old man more, reports in greater de-
tail. He said that Joshua's babbled words
were more like: *Tell them . . . zig when zag
. . . wrong way . . . master . . . my paintings
. . . my canvas . . . wrong to zigzag . . . tell*

'em . . . wrong. Over and over like that, at least in general."

Pete scratched his head. *"Tell them* sounds like a message, and *zig when zag* and *wrong way* sound as if Joshua was giving directions. Some way is wrong. But what's the right way?"

"Yes," Jupiter agreed, "that part seems missing. Only, you notice that the second time Hal used the word *wrong,* it was by itself without the word *way.*"

"What does that mean, Jupe?" Bob asked.

"I don't really know," Jupiter said lamely, "and there's another difference, too. Hal reports the words *tell them* the first time, and *tell 'em* the second time."

"We all say *tell 'em* when we mean *tell them,*" Pete said.

"I suppose that's all it is," Jupiter admitted.

Bob studied the words. *"Master* and *my paintings* could mean that Joshua thought his paintings were masterpieces — even though he was only an amateur. *My canvas,* and just *canvas,* are a painter's way of referring to his paintings."

"De Groot seems to think Joshua's paintings are good," Pete said.

Bob cried, "Maybe that's it! Maybe Joshua Cameron really was a good painter. A great painter, but eccentric, so he wouldn't show or sell his work! Maybe De Groot thinks he could sell Joshua's paintings for a whole lot of money!"

"That could be, but then Joshua's last words wouldn't be a message," Jupiter pointed out. "I'm sure there is a message, and one thing bothers me — why did Joshua say to tell *them?* Who is *them?*"

"The Countess and Mr. Marechal," Pete suggested.

"Mr. Marechal is only the Countess's estate manager," Jupiter analyzed. "Would Joshua lump them together as *them?* Wouldn't he give the message just for his sister, and say tell *her?* Or if it's for someone else, say tell *him?* Unless he wanted to leave a message for more than one person. Maybe for a gang?"

"A gang?" Pete gaped.

"A gang of crooks, maybe? Or smugglers?" Jupiter said. "Old Joshua kept to himself and never left the cottage — almost as if he were scared. Maybe he was hiding out!"

"And De Groot is one of the gang," Pete guessed, "looking for some loot, or for something smuggled into the country!"

"That would explain De Groot's search of the adobe when he locked us in last night," Jupiter said, "while Bob's idea that Joshua's paintings are really valuable, wouldn't. De Groot wouldn't have smashed everything in the adobe if he was hunting for twenty paintings." Jupiter stopped, a worried expression on his face.

"What is it, Jupe?" Bob asked.

"I'm not sure," the First Investigator said slowly. "While I was talking about last night at the adobe, something suddenly seemed wrong. At the back of my mind I feel I'm missing a fact, but I can't put my finger on it."

"I can't think of anything wrong last night," Pete said.

"Perhaps not," Jupiter said. "Anyway, I think we now have enough deductions to go to Mr. Marechal and try to get him to let us continue. At least, Pete and I will go."

"What do I do?" Bob demanded.

"We still want to find those paintings, Records. I'm not ruling out your idea that they may be good after all, and may be what De Groot wants," Jupiter explained. "You'll go and try again to talk to Skinny Norris. Learn where he got that one painting."

FAILURE!

The Cliff House Motel was an elegant resort establishment on the Pacific Ocean a mile south of Rocky Beach. Pete and Jupiter parked their bikes and walked into the glittering main lobby. A tall, severe-looking man seated at the registration desk watched them suspiciously.

"May I ask your business here, boys?" the man said.

Pete became nervous, but Jupiter was not easily intimidated. The stout boy drew himself up as tall as possible, and when he spoke his voice had a rich English accent!

"Announce us to the Countess, my good man," Jupiter said, looking down his nose at the clerk. "Jupiter Jones the Fourth, and Mr. Peter Crenshaw. You may also inform Monsieur Marechal we are here."

Pete could barely keep from laughing. He had seen Jupe's act before, but the desk clerk hadn't. The man hesitated uncertainly. Jupiter sounded for all the world like some English lord.

"On second thought," Jupiter said, "if you will be so kind as to inform me of Armand's room number, we shall present ourselves personally."

"Er," the desk clerk said, "Mr. Marechal is in cottage ten. I'll get a bellboy . . ."

"I shouldn't bother, my good man," Jupiter said grandly. "I expect we shall manage. Come, Peter."

Still looking down his nose, Jupiter paraded majestically through the lobby and out the side door into the beautiful grounds of the elegant motel.

Once out of sight of the desk, Jupiter dropped his act and laughed. "Cottage ten is to the left by that sign, Pete."

"That act is going to get us into trouble someday," Pete said. "At least a punch in the nose!"

"I hardly think so. Employees in expensive places are easily intimidated. They have to be very careful not to offend anyone who might be important," Jupiter observed.

They followed a narrow path through hibiscus and camellia bushes. They could hear the motel guests swimming and laughing in the motel pool and conversing on the cocktail terrace. Single cottages, as well as larger units of less expensive rooms, were scattered throughout the secluded grounds.

"Here is cottage nine," Jupiter said, "which means that cottage ten will be next around this palm tree."

The boys came around the palm tree — and stopped. Someone was standing at a window of cottage ten, peering inside! As they watched, the snooper went to Mr. Marechal's door and tried to force it open.

"Jupe!" Pete burst out. "It's . . ."

Too loud, Pete's voice startled the snooper, who turned quickly to stare toward the boys.

"Skinny Norris!" Jupiter finished for Pete.

Their enemy's mouth dropped open for a moment, like a surprised scarecrow. Then, as the boys started toward him, Skinny whirled and dashed off through the heavy vegetation of the motel grounds.

"After him, Second!" Jupiter cried.

Pete went after the lanky youth, racing

among the palms and hibiscus. Jupiter realized that he himself had no chance of catching Skinny by direct pursuit. He analyzed the situation, and saw that Skinny would have to circle back on the far side of the pool if he was to escape through the front of the motel. With Pete cutting off his rear, Skinny had to go that way! Jupiter began to run directly toward the pool.

He reached the cocktail terrace, and puffed out onto the green concrete to pass the pool itself. He was watching across the pool for a glimpse of Skinny or Pete, and completely failed to see Mr. Marechal until the small, silver-haired estate manager was directly in front of him.

"Awwkk!" Jupiter cried, and stopped just before he would have run right into the man.

"Jupiter! What are you doing?" Mr. Marechal thundered. "Is this your detective method? To trample me?"

"Sir," Jupiter panted, "we just discovered Skinny Norris breaking into your cottage! Pete is pursuing him now, and I was attempting to intercept him!"

"That boy who had one of Joshua Cameron's paintings?"

"Yes, sir. If Pete can — "

At that moment, Pete came walking dejectedly around the pool from the direction of the main entrance.

"He got away," Pete said. "I'm sorry, Mr. Marechal."

"Unfortunate." Mr. Marechal frowned. "What on earth was he doing at my cottage?"

"Are the things we recovered for the Countess in your cottage, sir?" Jupiter asked. "Joshua Cameron's possessions?"

"Yes. But what would young Norris want with them? A stuffed owl? Silverware? Binoculars? What earthly . . ." Mr. Marechal broke off. He was looking at the terrace. "I think the Countess wants us to join her. She is concerned in this."

The boys saw the Countess at a table on the terrace. They followed Mr. Marechal to her. The Countess was worried.

"Are you in trouble, boys?"

Mr. Marechal quickly explained about Skinny Norris, and waved the boys to seats. "But you didn't come here to chase young Norris, eh? I presume you had some reason?"

"Let us stay on the case, sir," Pete blurted out. "We've — "

"We'd like to, boys, but . . ."

"We've made some deductions, sir," Jupiter hurried on, and he explained how they had concluded that Joshua Cameron had had something valuable, that someone knew this, that the missing paintings were involved somehow, and that old Joshua's last words were a message. "We think there are two possible explanations, sir. First, that perhaps old Joshua was a good painter after all, and his paintings would be worth a lot, and De Groot knows this. Or, second, that Joshua was secretly part of a gang, and has hidden some valuable loot or some smuggled treasure!"

"Gang?" the estate manager said. "You mean criminals? The Countess's brother? Preposterous, boys!"

"Still," the Countess said slowly, "this man De Groot does appear to want something, and he doesn't sound a pleasant man."

Jupiter said, "Joshua could have been a dupe, sir."

"Hmmmm," Mr. Marechal mused, looked at the Countess. "Old Joshua *was* eccentric. You may have hit on something, boys. If so, it is more dangerous than ever, and a police matter."

"But, Mr. Marechal," Jupiter protested, "we can help —!"

"Absolutely out of the question! I'm sorry. Good-by, boys."

Slowly, Pete and Jupiter got up and left the terrace. This time they had really failed!

A SUDDEN ATTACK

Jupiter and Pete walked slowly through the elegant motel lobby and out the front door to their bikes. They were so despondent that they didn't notice the doorman coming after them. As Jupe began to mount his bike, he felt a restraining hand on his arm.

"Are you two the investigators?" the doorman demanded.

Pete swallowed. "We . . ."

"Speak up, boys! Are you or aren't you?"

"Ye-yes, sir," Jupiter stammered.

"Follow me, then. Hurry up!"

The boys looked at each other, shrugged, and meekly followed the doorman back into the lobby. They saw the severe-looking man at the registration desk watching them, and bellboys staring at them from every exit. What had they done now? The doorman directed them into a small side room, and closed the door behind them.

The Countess sat alone inside the room.

"I had to see you before you left," she said, and smiled. "I hated to see you so disappointed after you'd worked so hard for us."

"You mean we can stay on the case!" Pete cried.

"Mr. Marechal has changed his mind, ma'am?" Jupiter asked.

"No, and he's probably right," the Countess said. "But you've shown me that you're intelligent and know what you're doing, and I think you are more responsible than Mr. Marechal imagines."

"We are, ma'am!" both boys exclaimed at once.

"I recall that your card says the Chief of Police believes in you," the Countess went on. "If I permit you to continue working for me, you'll promise to be careful?"

"We sure will!" Pete declared.

"Good," the Countess said, and her regal face became sad. "I must know if your deductions have any truth. As I told you, I did not know my brother well. He was an odd, secretive man. I . . . I never knew what he really did all those years. He never seemed to have a home, and he had some strange friends."

"He might only have been a dupe for crooks," Jupiter said.

"Better that than a real criminal, but even so . . ." The Countess sighed. "You seem to have done fine work up until now, and I think you will find the truth for me. I want to know the truth about my poor brother once and for all."

"Countess?" Jupiter said. "You didn't find anything in what we already recovered for you, did you?"

"Nothing, Jupiter. Whatever do you think this valuable something could be? If there is something."

"We don't know that yet," Jupiter admitted.

"But you feel Joshua hid it somewhere, and that his last words were a message to someone? To say where it was?"

"I'm sure of it," Jupiter said eagerly.

"Very well, but be careful. Especially of this De Groot, whoever he is. Don't make me regret allowing you to go on. When you know **more, return and report to me.**"

The regal lady smiled at the boys and dismissed them. Excited to be still on the case, they hurried out to their bikes.

As Pete and Jupiter scrambled up from Tunnel Two into Headquarters, they found Bob waiting for them.

"I've got news, fellows!" Bob announced the moment his two partners entered.

"So have we!" Pete said.

"We're back on the case, Records," Jupiter crowed, and told Bob all about what had happened at The Cliff House.

"So that's where Skinny drove up from in such a wild hurry," Bob said. "I thought he looked scared. Gosh, it's great we're still on the case!"

"You saw Skinny at his house, Records?" Jupiter asked. "And you have some news about him?"

"I sure do," Bob declared. "When he came home, he just ran into his house and stayed there. But I'd managed to have a talk with the Norrises' gardener before that, and I found out where Skinny is working."

"Is that important, Bob?" Pete asked.

"Where, Records?" Jupiter said.

"He's been working as an assistant to Mr. **Maxwell James!**"

Pete was puzzled. "Maxwell James? Is that supposed . . ."

"The famous artist!" Jupiter exclaimed, his eyes shining. "His paintings are known all over the world, and he does live right here in Rocky Beach!"

"In a big mansion, with a separate studio," Bob remembered. "It sure is a coincidence that we're looking for paintings, and Skinny is working for a famous painter."

"Too much coincidence, fellows," Jupiter said. "After lunch, I think we must pay a visit to Mr. Maxwell James."

They parked their bikes just outside the high iron gates to the estate of Mr. Maxwell James. They could see the stone towers of a large, castlelike house above the trees on the heavily wooded grounds. The iron gates were open, and no one seemed to be around in the afternoon sun.

"I guess we just walk in," Pete decided.

They went through the big gates, and started up a narrow, winding path through junglelike vegetation. All at once, a loud, chilling scream echoed through the grounds. A scream like a woman or child in great pain.

"What was that?" Bob whispered.

"I don't want to know," Pete moaned. "Let's go!"

The agonized scream came again. Somewhere to the left.

"Someone needs help!" Bob cried.

"Come on," Jupiter said. "Careful, and stay low!"

They moved cautiously through the tangled shrubbery. The chilling scream sounded again — directly in front of them! Jupiter parted some thick leaves, and they looked through the bushes at a small clearing.

A huge spotted cat crouched in the clearing!

Speechless, they looked at the green eyes that stared savagely at them. Even as they watched, the tawny cat opened its fanged mouth — and gave the high, agonized scream.

"A leopard!" Jupiter said. "Run!"

"NO!" Pete commanded. "Don't run, guys. Stand still!"

A voice spoke sharply from behind the boys. "So! I've caught you, have I? Don't try to get away."

They whirled to see a big, bearlike man with a red beard and thick red hair. The man's eyes were angry, and he held a gleaming spear with a narrow blade at least three feet long!

Looking for somewhere to escape, the boys turned back toward the enormous cat. With a sudden snarl, the leopard leaped straight at the boys!

THE HAUNTED PAINTINGS

The savage leopard hurled through the air at the boys — and seemed to strike an invisible wall! It fell back to the ground. Bruised, it slunk away into the small clearing and crouched there, staring at them with its green eyes.

"How . . . ?" Bob began, his voice shaking.

Pete reached out through the leaves in front of them. Only a foot away, his hand struck the invisible wall.

"Glass!" the Second Investigator said. "The leopard's in a big glass cage. We're so close to the glass, we can't see it. That whole clearing is inside a glass cage!"

"Of course it is," the red-bearded man said behind them. "You didn't think anyone would let an African leopard roam loose in Rocky Beach, did you?"

"I . . . I guess we weren't thinking," said Jupe.

Bob asked, "Why do you have it in that glass cage, sir?"

"How else could I study the animal's movements, the play of its muscles, the way it walks, sits, screams?" the bearded man said.

"You're the artist!" Jupiter realized. "Mr. Maxwell James!"

"And you're painting the leopard," Bob guessed.

"I am painting many African themes. For example, this spear here. It's a most unusual spear, with a very long, thin blade. A Masai spear. Made for lion hunting, but it has other uses!" And Mr. James aimed the long, savage spear straight at the boys. "Now, what have you three trespassers been doing in my studio!"

"We haven't been in your studio," Pete said hotly, "and we're not trespassers!"

"Then what are you doing sneaking around on my land?"

Jupiter said, "We're detectives, Mr. James.

We came here to talk to you about your assistant, Skinny Norris. But now — "

"Norris? That young scamp! Now I'm sure you three are up to no good! March into my house. I shall call the police!"

The artist leveled the menacing spear. Glumly, the boys marched into the big, castle-like house. Mr. James herded them into a book-lined study.

"If you're calling the police, sir," Jupiter said, "ask for Chief Reynolds. He knows us."

"The Chief knows you?" Mr. James hesitated.

Jupiter seized the chance. "If you would examine our cards, sir, it would help."

The stocky leader of the boys took out their cards and gave them to the artist. Mr. James read them with a scowl.

"This does appear to be the Chief's signature," Mr. James said grudgingly.

"Call Alfred Hitchcock, the motion picture director, if you still don't believe us!" Pete said.

"Alfred?" Mr. James glared. "Now you have made a mistake! I *will* call my good friend Alfred, to expose you!"

The artist picked up the telephone and dialed. He asked for Mr. Hitchcock. "Alfred? Max James, here. I have in my house a trio of young trespassers! They . . . What? Yes, those are their names, I have some cards of theirs. How did you know? . . . I see, yes. . . . They are, are they? . . . Very well, Alfred. Good-by."

The artist hung up, and considered the boys. "So, you *are* detectives, after all. Alfred informs me that you are honest boys, and quite clever. No spear seems needed."

Mr. James leaned his Masai spear in a corner.

"Mr. Hitchcock has helped us greatly," Jupiter said primly.

"So he said," Mr. James stated. "However, he also says that involvement with you three is to be avoided at all costs, if I value my peaceful life, and that you tend to have somewhat wild imaginations. Hmmmm. Perhaps I need imaginations."

"To solve the mystery in your studio, sir?" Jupiter asked.

"What? How do you know there's a mystery in my studio?"

"You accused us of doing something in your studio," the First Investigator said. "So something has happened there. And you said you might need imagination, so whatever has happened must be a mystery."

"That is clever deduction, yes."

"Would it have anything to do with a stolen painting?"

"How did you know that? Not stolen, but taken without permission and returned. I fired the culprit. But that has nothing to do with my mystery. To put it bluntly, boys, I seem to have acquired some haunted paintings!"

"Haunted paintings?" Bob and Pete exclaimed.

"I can think of no other explanation," Mr. James said. "My studio is some distance from this house. The last two mornings, I arrived to work — and found that paintings had moved during the night. Other objects were out of place, too. Nothing missing, and no chaos — just a few things where I didn't leave them."

Jupiter said, "Are the 'haunted' paintings like the one painting that was taken and returned, sir?"

"Why, yes! They are all ones I bought from a junkyard."

"Then I think I can explain what has been happening," Jupiter said, and told about Joshua Cameron, the Countess and Mr. Marechal, and De Groot. "So I think that someone has been entering your studio to examine the paintings!"

"I see," Mr. James said. "There is only one problem. At night, there is no way in or out of my studio! At night, it is a completely locked room!"

THE BOYS SET A TRAP

"A locked room?" Bob cried.

"Absolutely no way to get in or out," Mr. James declared. "Would you boys care to inspect the studio?"

"Yes, sir!" Pete said.

They followed Mr. James out of the big stone house and across the overgrown estate, past the leopard in its glass cage. The studio was also a stone building, with heavily barred windows and a massive iron door. As they went in, Jupiter paused to study the modern, tamperproof lock on the iron door.

"It is guaranteed to take an expert an hour to pick that lock, my boy," Mr. James observed, "and there are no marks on it anyway."

Inside, Jupiter turned first to inspect the hinges of the iron door. They were on the inside, and untouched.

"There's only the one door, Jupiter," Mr. James said.

It was a large studio, equipped with racks for everything. Light poured in through two casement windows and a big skylight. The windows, which opened inward, were solidly barred on the outside. The skylight did not open at all. There was no fireplace or stove. A small exhaust fan was built high into the rear wall; an electric cord dangled from it down to a socket near the floor. The floor itself was solid stone, with no basement underneath. There were no hollow places in the floor or in any of the walls. A simple, solid, fortresslike room, with no way in or out except through the single door.

"And I lock that every night," Mr. James said.

"Gosh," Pete said. "Maybe earthquakes made the things move. We get little ones all the time."

"No, Pete," Mr. James said. "The paintings weren't just moved, they were in the wrong slots in their racks."

"These racks here, Mr. James?" Jupiter said.

He pointed to a large rack filled with completed paintings.

"No, that's my work," the artist said. "The canvases I bought from the junkyard are over in that rack."

Mr. James indicated a smaller rack that held mostly blank canvases. Jupiter saw the edges of two of Joshua Cameron's last paintings.

"May we see all the paintings, Mr. James?" he asked.

"Of course. Help me out with them, boys."

A few minutes later, all twenty paintings were spread around the studio, leaning on the walls and racks.

"Why do you have them in that rack for unused canvases, Mr. James?" Jupiter questioned.

"Because I bought them to paint over, and use for my own work. Most artists do that. I'm always looking for used canvases. Last week I dropped by your uncle's junkyard for the first time, on the odd chance that there might be some old paintings in stock, and I found these twenty."

"You'll paint over them?" Bob said.

Mr. James nodded.

"Then," Jupiter said, "you don't think they're very good? They're not worth anything?"

"Not to me, Jupiter, and I never heard of Joshua Cameron," Mr. James said. "But, as a matter of fact, these paintings show very good technique. Cameron was an extremely expert painter, amazingly so. It's indeed odd that he was totally unknown."

"He never showed or sold his work," Pete explained.

"An eccentric, you said, yes." Mr. James nodded. "Alas, the world may have lost a fine painter."

"His work could have been great?" Jupiter asked. "I mean, sir, could someone have thought these paintings were valuable, and wanted to buy them?"

"Perhaps." Mr. James looked thoughtfully at the paintings. "But I doubt it. It takes more than the finest skill to make a great artist. You must have 'feeling,' 'style,' something that makes your work different from anyone else's work. You notice how each of these paintings looks very different? As if each one were done by a different artist? Most artists have a style of their own. Joshua Cameron doesn't seem to have had."

"You mean most artists paint the same all the time?" Bob asked.

"They change, but not much. These paintings have been done twenty different ways, none of them very original. Mr. Cameron imitated the work of other artists instead of expressing a distinctive style of his own. No knowledgeable buyer of art would think these paintings were valuable."

"May we examine them, sir?" Jupiter asked.

"Go right ahead, Jupiter."

The boys studied the paintings. There were no frames, just the canvases stretched on wood. In the end, they found nothing.

"There sure isn't anything hidden in them," Pete decided, "and no messages I can see."

"No," Jupiter agreed, staring at the paintings. In each one, the cottage in Remuda Canyon seemed to stare back. Then Jupiter bent down close to one. "Fellows! They seem to be numbered! This is number one, and . . ."

The boys hurriedly inspected the paintings again, and found a number on each one — painted right on the picture in a corner. They moved them until they were in order. Then they stood back and looked at them again. So did Mr. James.

The paintings were now lined up so that the largest close-up of the cottage was first, and the view from farthest away was last.

"I don't get any message," Pete said after a time.

"Neither do I," Bob agreed.

"You know," said Jupiter at last, "the way they're painted, the cottage looks like it's shrinking. The trees in the front, the rocks, the canvas chair — all stay the same size in each painting. But the house gets smaller until about all you can see in the last one is that porch awning."

"You're right, Jupe!" said Bob. "It does look like the house is shrinking instead of just being farther away. But what could that mean?"

"So now you have the mystery of the shrinking house," Mr. James said, smiling, "to go with my haunted paintings!"

"I *know* there's something important about these paintings," Jupiter said, "and that's why someone has been in here moving them at night."

"No one can get in here, Jupiter," Mr. James said.

Jupiter shook his head firmly. "There is no

such thing as a locked room in which things move by themselves."

The First Investigator sat down on a long, rug-covered bench, and looked all around the studio. Mr. James sat on a couch. Bob and Pete each took armchairs.

"If we could catch the person who has been breaking in here," said Jupe, "we might find out why the paintings are important."

"How are we going to do that?" Pete asked.

Jupiter got up from the rug-covered bench and opened the door to the studio's single closet. It was lined with shelves filled with cans, brushes, and other equipment, and had solid stone walls.

"There's only one way," Jupiter said. "One of us must hide in this closet and see if anyone gets in the studio tonight!"

"All right, Jupiter. I'll hide in the closet," Mr. James said.

"No, sir. You have to lock the door and go away. I'm certain you would be watched. An intruder would never come in unless he was sure you had locked up and gone."

"Gee," Bob said, "I have to work for my dad tonight."

"And I," Jupiter decided, "must be outside to observe."

Pete groaned aloud. "Just wait, fellows, I'll think of something I have to do somewhere else tonight!"

"We must know what's been happening, Pete," Jupiter said.

"Sure, I want to know how things got moved in a locked studio, too." Pete shivered. "But I don't think I want to be in here when I find out!"

"We'll be outside, Pete," Mr. James assured him.

Jupiter outlined the plan for the evening. Then all three boys went home, and Jupe and Pete made arrangements to stay with Mr. James overnight. After dinner, the two sneaked back into Mr. James's estate and silently made their way through the shadowed jungle to the studio. They hid outside for a while, carefully looking and listening for signs of the mysterious intruder. When all seemed safe, Pete darted into the studio and slipped into the closet. With the door ajar a few inches, he could see both windows and half the room. Outside, Jupiter took up a position in a clump of bushes from which he could watch the entrance to the studio.

Just before sunset, as Jupe had planned, Maxwell James came noisily down the path from the main house. The artist checked that

Pete was in the closet, straightened up a few things in the studio, and locked the windows. Going outside, he clanged the iron door shut behind him and locked it. Then he clomped noisily back to the house to wait for dark, when he would join Jupiter.

A LOCKED ROOM

Through the crack in the closet door, Pete watched it grow dark outside the two barred windows. He was cramped in a sitting position, but didn't want to move for fear of making a noise.

An hour passed.

Nothing happened. The closet grew hot and stuffy. Pete wondered if Jupiter and Mr. James were alert outside. His legs were going to sleep, and that made him nervous.

After a while the tall Second Investigator was hungry. He had brought some sand-

wiches, and now he cautiously opened one
and tried to eat without making a sound.

Another hour passed.

Moonlight filtered through the heavy foli-
age of the trees, casting weird shadows.
Jupiter and Mr. James crouched behind thick
bushes and watched the locked door.

By 10 P.M. they had seen nothing.

The studio remained dark and silent.

No one moved in the junglelike grounds
of Mr. James's estate.

Nothing had happened at all — nothing out
of the way, at least. The leopard paced and
growled in its dark glass cage. A few insects
chirred, and small night creatures rustled in
the underbrush.

Jupiter shifted his weight restlessly and
sighed.

Nothing happened.

Pete battled sleep. Cramped in the closet,
hot and shut in, he felt his eyes grow heavy.
Something seemed to be making his head feel
light, sending waves of sleep over him.

He fought, but his eyes kept closing. Twice
he forced himself out of a momentary doze.
The third time he came awake, from a longer

doze, he realized what was making his head feel so light — fumes!

The closet was full of cans of paint and thinner and solvents. Their fumes were filling the closet. Because of the heat, the silence, and the heady fumes, Pete couldn't fight off sleep.

He dozed. How long, he didn't know. But when he came slowly awake again — it was in the studio!

Something!

Pete shook his head to clear it. Was he awake? Or was he still asleep? His mind seemed to swim in a thick haze.

It, something, moved out in the studio. A thin shape floating in a moonlit glow. An eerie figure that seemed to pick up a painting and float with it to a barred window, where the painting vanished into thin air!

The ghostly figure hovered near the window for what seemed like hours. Pete desperately tried to wake up enough to do something.

A shimmering, twisting painting appeared near the odd figure again. The shape floated back with it to the rack, and took another painting to the barred window.

Pete tried to stand.

His legs wouldn't move!

The hazy figure floated back toward him.

Pete tried to cry out.

Jupiter and Mr. James heard the muffled cry.

"Help!"

The cry was faint — inside the studio!

"Quick, Jupiter!" Mr. James said.

They leaped up and ran toward the iron door. The studio was still dark. They heard no more sounds from inside as they reached the door. Mr. James fumbled with his key and missed the lock the first time. At last the artist inserted the key and unlocked the door. Flinging it open, he rushed into the dark studio.

"Lights, Jupiter! There on the wall near the door!"

Jupiter found the switch and turned on the lights.

The studio was empty.

Mr. James and Jupiter ran to the closet. Pete still sat there on the floor. His eyes were open, but he seemed in a daze.

"Thunderation! The solvent and thinner fumes!" Mr. James muttered. "Get him out, Jupiter."

Together, they helped Pete up. The Second Investigator's legs were asleep, and Jupiter and Mr. James had to walk him back and forth until circulation returned. Pete's head cleared rapidly in the fresh air of the studio.

"Wow," Pete said, "I just couldn't stay awake. But I saw it! Something weird, like a ghost!"

"Look!" Jupiter cried.

On the studio floor near the rear window lay one of Joshua Cameron's paintings! The window was open.

"The ghost did it!" Pete shivered, and sat down on the rug-covered bench as if he needed the support of something solid. Then he described how the ghost had floated back and forth with the paintings.

"Someone was in here, all right," said Jupiter, "but it wasn't any ghost. I can't accept a ghost that just happens to be interested in Joshua Cameron's paintings."

"I know I saw a ghost!" said Pete stubbornly.

"Now, Second, let's be logical. You were half asleep and dazed by those solvent fumes. You saw someone here and just assumed he was a ghost."

"Then how did he get in here?" asked Mr. James. "No one but a ghost could have slipped between those window bars, and we didn't see anyone approach the studio door."

"Ergo, he came in another way," said Jupe. He looked carefully around the studio. Suddenly his eyes gleamed.

"There!" he exclaimed. "Up there!"

Pete and Mr. James looked where Jupe was pointing, high on the back wall. There, where the built-in exhaust fan was supposed to be, a small square hole gaped open to the night. The once slack electrical cord now ran tautly from the socket up to the opening — and out.

Jupiter walked over to the cord and tugged gently on it. A scraping sound came from the other side of the wall.

"Your fan wasn't bolted in securely, Mr. James," said Jupe triumphantly. "Our 'ghost' pulled it out and simply let it dangle outside by its cord while he climbed in."

"But Jupe!" protested Pete. "That hole is barely more than a foot square. Who could get through that?"

"Someone who is very small or very thin, obviously," answered Jupe.

Mr. James shook his head in amazement. "I should have known there'd be a logical explanation. I never thought to check the fan bolts."

"Neither did I," admitted Jupe ruefully. Jupe hated to make mistakes, and was now annoyed with himself for failing to investigate more thoroughly earlier in the day. He scowled up at the fan opening. Then, gradually, his expression changed to one of puzzlement.

"There's only one problem," said Jupe, almost to himself. "We answered Pete's call very quickly — in a matter of seconds. I don't see how anyone had time to climb back up through that hole and escape unseen."

Mr. James looked around and shrugged. "Well, there's certainly no one here now!"

"Yeah, Jupe," agreed Pete.

Jupiter glanced at Pete — and then stared!

"What is it, Jupe?" Pete asked nervously.

"I think I know the answer," Jupiter said quietly. "I know where our 'ghost' is!"

"Where?" Pete cried.

"Look down," Jupiter said. "You're sitting on him!"

Pete leaped up as if stung. He stared back at the long, heavy, rug-covered bench he had been sitting on. Jupiter's voice was loud as he spoke:

"All right, you can come out of that chest now!"

There was a silence. Then the rug rose slowly in the air and fell back as the "bench" was revealed to be a long chest with a lid that swung up. The boys and Mr. James blinked at the scared figure that emerged from the chest.

"Skinny Norris!" Pete cried.

THE LOST MASTERPIECE

Skinny Norris sat pale and dejected in the corner of the studio. Pete stood guard over him.

"How did you know he was in the chest?" Maxwell James asked Jupiter.

"He disarranged the rug when he climbed in," said Jupe. "A corner of the chest showed, and I realized that it wasn't a bench, as I'd assumed earlier. And, since there was no place else to hide here, I knew the intruder had to be in the chest!"

"A logical deduction," Mr. James said, and turned to Skinny Norris. "So, it's not enough that you were fired for taking a painting without permission? You come back and break into my studio, eh? Why?"

"You shouldn't have fired me," Skinny said defiantly. "I brought it back."

"That was not the point. You took what did not belong to you, without asking," Mr. James thundered. "What have you been doing in this studio these last nights? What is your concern with Joshua Cameron's paintings?"

"Wouldn't you all like to know," Skinny jeered.

"You were passing them out the window to someone, and then getting them back," Jupiter said. "Who were you passing them to, and what did he want with them?"

"I'm not telling you anything!"

"Was it De Groot, the art dealer, out there?" Pete asked.

"I don't know anyone named De Groot," Skinny said.

"You refuse to cooperate?" Mr. James said ominously. "We'll see, young man. This is not 'borrowing' a painting. This is breaking and entering, a serious crime. We'll see what the police think about it, eh?"

"P-p-police?" Skinny stammered. "No, my dad'll kill me! I didn't mean . . ."

It was Pete who caught a glimpse of the face at the rear window.

"Jupe!" Pete cried. "Someone's at the . . ."

A muffled voice rasped, "Do not move, any of you! I have a gun! Remain where you are. Norris, hurry!"

Neither Jupiter nor Pete recognized the muffled voice.

"Don't move, boys," Mr. James said. "He might shoot."

Behind them, the iron door clanged shut as Skinny escaped. They heard the man at the window run away in the night.

"He's gone!" Pete cried.

"So is Skinny," Jupiter groaned. "Just when we had him!"

"Never mind, boys," Mr. James said. "We can find Skinny again. Either he'll give me a satisfactory explanation — or I'll report him to the police."

"Well, we found out that Skinny was the intruder, and we know he's in league with someone else," said Jupe, "but we don't know who or why. What could that man out there want with old Joshua's paintings?"

"Skinny passed them out the window one at a time," Pete observed, "but the man passed them back. So it's not the paintings themselves he wants. Unless he's been switching the paintings! Stealing the real ones and passing back substitutes!"

"No," Mr. James said, "that painting on the floor is one of the real ones. No doubt of it."

Jupiter bent down to study the one painting lying on the floor near the window. He shook his head hopelessly.

"If the paintings form some kind of message, a code, I can't . . . Mr. James!"

Jupiter was peering very closely at a corner of the painting. Mr. James came over to him.

"This corner of the painting appears to be wet!" the First Investigator said.

"Wet?" Mr. James echoed. The artist touched the canvas. "Why, it *is* wet! Someone's tampered with it, retouched it!"

"Why would anyone retouch them?" Pete wondered.

Mr. James rubbed at the wet corner of the canvas. "Well, perhaps someone wanted to see if there was another painting hidden under Joshua Cameron's picture. He removed a layer of paint in the corner, then retouched it to hide what he'd done."

Jupiter looked as if he had seen a vision. "Something *under* old Joshua's painting? Mr. James, may we use the telephone? I have to make a call. It's still not too late!"

* * *

A half an hour later, Jupiter, Pete, and Mr. James were standing out in front of the main house when Professor Carswell and Hal drove up. Jupe introduced Mr. James to the Carswells.

"What's up, Jupe?" Hal wanted to know.

"Come on back to Mr. James's studio," the First Investigator said.

Inside the studio, Pete and Jupiter had taken all of Joshua Cameron's paintings out of the rack again. Hal and his dad saw them as soon as they entered.

"You've found them all!" Hal cried.

"This is fine work, boys," Professor Carswell said. "Have you told the Countess yet? She'll be most pleased."

"Not yet, sir," Jupiter said. "We called you because we have an idea about all that's been going on. We think we know what is so valuable that everyone wants it."

"We do?" Pete said.

"Yes, we do," Jupiter said. "Hal, do you remember that gold frame in the adobe? You said there was a painting in it once."

"Gold frame?" Professor Carswell repeated. "I don't recall seeing a painting in a gold frame, Hal."

"It was when Mr. Cameron first came to the cottage, Dad," Hal explained. "I sort of saw it by accident one day. Old Joshua said it was an imitation, a print, and he was going to get rid of it. I never saw it again. The frame was empty in the adobe."

"Can you describe it, Hal?" Jupiter asked.

Hal scratched his head. "Well, it was a mountain, some horses, what looked like palm trees, and some people in front of a grass hut. Only the mountain was purple, the horses were blue, the palm trees were yellow, and the people were red!"

"What!" Mr. James cried. The artist's eyes were very excited. "Are you sure the painting looked like that, Hal?"

"Sure I am. All those crazy colors."

"You recognize that painting, sir?" Jupiter said quickly.

"Wait!" Mr. James said, and went to rummage among many large books on a shelf. He opened one and flipped the pages. "There! Is this the painting you saw, Hal?"

Hal looked at the picture in the book. They all did.

"It sure is!" Hal declared. "Exactly!"

"Then what you saw was a print of a very famous painting by a great French painter named François Fortunard. A masterpiece, boys, but one that no longer exists. It was **destroyed by the Nazis when they occupied**

131

France during World War II. They hated François Fortunard's work. It was a terrible tragedy for art. Only" — Mr. James had an odd look on his face — "this painting was privately owned, and I didn't know any prints had been made."

"I don't think any prints were made, sir," Jupiter said. "I think it was never destroyed, and Joshua Cameron had it!"

"Wow!" Pete exclaimed. "How much would it be worth?"

"Any Fortunard would be worth a fortune," Mr. James said, "but one that had supposedly been destroyed might be worth much more. Perhaps half a million dollars! Jupiter, you really think . . . ?"

"I'm certain old Joshua had something very valuable that he hid somewhere," Jupiter said. "He used the word *master* in his delirious babbling. I think he meant *masterpiece*, and that is why someone wants his paintings — and thinks something is underneath one of them!"

"The Fortunard *under* one of those!" Mr. James cried, staring at the twenty paintings of the old man. "Then let's look!"

"Wait a minute!" said Professor Carswell. "How can you look under the cottage paintings without damaging whatever may be underneath?"

"It's tricky," admitted Mr. James. "But I have studied restoration techniques and know how to do this safely."

The bearded artist got some solvent, a soft cloth, and some other equipment. He carefully rubbed off a small spot on a cottage painting. When he found nothing underneath, he retouched the spot and went on to another picture. A half an hour later he stood up sadly.

"There's nothing hidden under any of these paintings, Jupiter," Mr. James said. "I guess you're wrong. The Fortunard was destroyed."

Jupiter bit his lip. "I was so sure, sir! These paintings have to be the key to something very valuable!"

"Perhaps, Jupiter," Mr. James said, "but there must be some other answer. The paintings are just what they seem to be."

"I suppose Hal and I had better take them, then," Professor Carswell said. "We'll return them to the Countess tomorrow, and she will reimburse you, Mr. James."

The boys helped load the twenty paintings into Professor Carswell's car, and the Professor and Hal drove home.

"You boys might as well sleep here," Mr. James said. "It's too late to take you home now. Maybe you can think of some other explanation for why those paintings seem valuable. And perhaps Skinny Norris can tell us more," Mr. James added grimly. "Tomorrow, we'll find Skinny and make him talk."

A DISAPPEARANCE!

In the morning, Jupiter had to go home to man the office of the junkyard while Uncle Titus went off with Hans and Konrad on a sudden buying trip. So only Pete drove with Mr. James to Skinny Norris's house.

"I don't see Skinny's car, Mr. James," Pete observed.

"Perhaps his parents can tell us where he is," the artist said.

It was Mrs. Norris who answered their ring. Skinny's mother's face fell as she saw them.

"I thought . . ." Mrs. Norris began, and then she looked angrily at Pete. "Have you been doing something to Skinner, Peter Crenshaw! Whenever Skinner becomes involved with you and your ridiculous friend Jupiter Jones, something seems to happen to him! What have you done now?"

"The boys have done nothing, Mrs. Norris," Mr. James said bluntly. "It is rather the opposite, and if unfortunate things happen to your son when he is involved with Pete and Jupiter, I suspect the fault lies with Skinner!"

"Just who are you?" Mrs. Norris snapped.

"My name is Maxwell James, madam."

"The artist Skinner was working for? Why did you fire him so unfairly?"

"Did your son say I fired him unfairly?" Mr. James said. "It seems that young Skinner is given to lying even to you." The artist told Mrs. Norris how he had fired Skinny for taking a painting without permission.

Mrs. Norris looked unhappy. "Skinner didn't tell me that. I'm sorry, Mr. James. Skinner does seem to have poor judgment at times, and I know that Peter and Jupiter drive him wild."

"I'm afraid your son is simply jealous," Mr. James said. "Now, may we speak to him?"

"He's not home, Mr. James."

"Where is he then? I assure you, it is a serious matter I wish to talk to him about," the artist said.

Skinny's mother suddenly looked miserable. "I .... I don't know where Skinner is, Mr. James. He ... he didn't come home at all last night!"

"He's been out all night?" Pete exclaimed.

"Yes," Mrs. Norris said, her eyes scared now. "When you rang, I thought it was Skinner, or someone who knew where he was. His father has already gone to the police."

"Mrs. Norris," Pete asked, "did Skinny tell you anything about what he's been doing after he got fired by Mr. James?"

"I've tried to think," Skinny's mother said, "but all I can remember is that he was working for some man, and that he said something was the key to a fortune. I have no idea what Skinner meant, but I'm terribly worried now. If a fortune is involved, anything could have happened to Skinner!"

"I wouldn't worry, Mrs. Norris," Mr. James said. "I'm afraid Skinny got into some trouble with me last night. I think I scared him by mentioning the police, and he probably has simply hidden somewhere to avoid being caught."

"I hope so, Mr. James," Skinny's mother

said, "but I can't help worrying. A man in a blue car has been loitering around here. Skinner was seen talking to the man, and we discovered that our telephone has been tapped. I'm so afraid that Skinner has been kidnapped!"

Bob showed up at the junkyard just as Uncle Titus returned from his buying trip. Jupiter was now free for a while, and the two boys retired to Headquarters to puzzle over their case.

Jupiter quickly related the events of the night at Mr. James's studio. Bob listened eagerly. He was as disappointed as the other boys had been when he learned that nothing had been found under the twenty paintings.

"Then Joshua didn't have the valuable Fortunard?" Bob said sadly. "It *was* destroyed by the Nazis. Joshua had a print."

"No, I believe Joshua did have the Fortunard, and hid it," Jupiter said stubbornly. "When he used the word *master* in his babbling, I'm convinced he was trying to say *masterpiece*. Hal stumbled on it, and Joshua pretended it was a print. Then Joshua hid the painting so no one else would see it. When he got sick, he tried to leave a message telling where it was. A disguised message, so Hal and his dad wouldn't know what he was really saying."

Jupiter took out the sheet of paper with Joshua Cameron's last words on it, and spread it on the table. "Now, *zig when zag* and *wrong way* could be directions. However, the second time Joshua used the word *wrong*, he used it alone. Maybe it's not a direction. Maybe it's telling us to look for something wrong. Something that ought to be different than it is."

"You mean something *done* the wrong way?" Bob asked. "Maybe something that zigs when it ought to zag? Looks wrong?"

"Exactly, Records," Jupiter said. "I'm sure that *master* means *masterpiece*, and the fact that old Joshua kept saying *my paintings*, *my canvas*, and *canvas* must mean that his own paintings are a key to the message. There is something about his paintings that should tell us where the masterpiece is!"

"But what, Jupe?" Bob stared at the words on the paper. "You and Pete looked at those paintings pretty closely."

Jupiter shook his head unhappily. "I admit I'm stumped at the moment. But we still have a clue to work with — the way the cottage seems to shrink in those paintings. Why did old Joshua paint the houses smaller and smaller, while leaving everything else in the pictures the same size?"

Bob thought. "Maybe he was trying to tell us to get the cottage out of the picture, Jupe? Maybe it's hidden *under* the cottage?"

"Well . . ." Jupiter said slowly. "That's possible. But, then, you'd think he would omit the cottage entirely in the last painting."

"How about in one of the trees? In something that stays the same in all the pictures? Maybe if we look, we'll find just one thing that's always the same!"

"That could be, too, Records. I want to take a closer look at those paintings after Pete and Mr. James get back from talking to Skinny Norris. Maybe Skinny will tell them the answer anyway."

"Gosh, you think he will, First?"

"Perhaps, but I'm not optimistic, Bob. I doubt that whoever hired Skinny would tell him much."

"*I* sure wouldn't," Bob agreed.

"Meanwhile," Jupiter went on, "something else puzzles me a lot."

"What's that, Jupe?"

"Do you remember Hal telling us that old Joshua once said that he was the most expensive painter in the world, but that no one knew it? Hal said Joshua laughed after saying that. Why did he laugh, and what did he mean?"

"Maybe Joshua meant that his paintings are expensive because they're a key to the valuable masterpiece by Fortunard."

"I thought of that," Jupiter replied, "but it sounds to me as if Joshua was speaking more generally — as if his own paintings were expensive but unknown."

"Well, Mr. James said Joshua was technically very good, and De Groot seems to think the paintings are good."

"But Mr. James also said Joshua had no style of his own, so his work isn't good — and an art dealer should know that. I think De Groot is fooling us. I don't think De Groot is an art dealer at all!"

"Gosh, what is he, then, Jupe? A gang member?"

"I'm not sure," Jupiter admitted, "but I'm convinced that De Groot knows that Joshua had the famous Fortunard, and wants it!"

"You think it's De Groot old Joshua tried to leave a message for?" Bob wondered.

"Could be, Records," Jupiter said. "I think..."

They both heard the scrambling down in

Tunnel Two. The trap door opened and Pete climbed up. The tall Second Investigator was grim and serious as he looked at his friends.

"Skinny's disappeared, fellows! His mother thinks maybe he's been kidnapped!"

"Kidnapped!" Bob cried.

"By whom, Pete?" Jupiter asked quickly.

"The Norrises don't know, First. But Skinny's mother says she saw the blue coupe hanging around, and Skinny talking to the man in it."

"De Groot!" Bob said fiercely.

"Mrs. Norris says their telephone was tapped, too," Pete added. "That must have been what De Groot was doing the day we saw him, Jupe. The day he caught us."

"Yes," Jupiter agreed. "Does Mrs. Norris know what Skinny was doing, or who he was working with?"

"No, First," Pete said. "Except that Skinny was working for some man, and Skinny said that something was the key to a fortune!"

Jupiter thought hard. "Fellows, Skinny's job was to pass those paintings out the studio window to whoever he was working for. That proves that those paintings really *are* the key to everything! And his kidnapping could mean only one thing — that Skinny knows too much, and someone wants to keep him silent. Someone named De Groot, I'll bet!"

"Poor Skinny," Bob said. "He sure can get into trouble."

"Yes," Jupiter said, "and if we want to get him out of trouble, we have to solve the message of old Joshua's paintings quickly! Let's go to Remuda Canyon!"

TRAPPED!

As the boys biked out to Professor Carswell's house, Pete told the others that Mr. James had gone to the police to report the incident at his studio the night before.

"Mr. Norris was already with the police about Skinny being missing," Pete added.

"They'll be looking for De Groot's blue coupe," Jupiter said. "But if we can solve the riddle of the last words and the paintings, I think we'll find De Groot faster."

"You think De Groot has solved the message?" Bob asked.

"I think he must be at least close to it. That's why he's probably holding Skinny,"

Jupiter said. "To keep Skinny from talking to anyone before he gets the masterpiece."

When they arrived at the big frame house in the canyon, the boys saw Hal standing on the porch of the cottage. Hal ran off the porch to meet them. He was agitated.

"Someone was out here again this morning!" Hal cried when he reached the Investigators. "He tore up the whole cottage."

"Were the twenty paintings in the cottage?" Jupiter asked.

"No. They were in our house. We tried to call the Countess and Mr. Marechal this morning, but they were out," Hal explained. "Dad drove over to their motel to talk to the Countess in person, to tell her that we had the paintings but that someone is still searching."

"Did you see anyone around this morning?" Jupiter asked.

"Yes, we did," Hal said. "Over near the garage. Just a glimpse, but it was a man. He ran off toward the barranca again, and that's when we found the cottage ransacked."

"Let's look around the garage," Pete said.

"Maybe he dropped something," Bob added.

They all went to the garage behind the big house and spread out to search the ground.

They found nothing. Dejected, they gathered outside the garage.

"There certainly aren't any signs of him," Bob said.

"No," Jupiter said. "Not even any footprints. Let's go to the cottage. I want to see . . ."

The strange noise reached them thinly in the late morning sun. They all looked at each other. It was an odd sound, like the strangled groaning of some small animal.

"Wh-what is it, fellows?" Hal stammered.

"Shhhh!" Jupiter said softly.

The strangled noise was faint and yet close. It sounded as if someone were trying to talk with his face pressed against the ground. An indistinct mumble. Then something banged inside the garage.

"It's the garage!" Pete cried.

"Someone's in there!" Bob exclaimed.

Pete ran up to the main door of the garage and tried to tug it open. It didn't budge.

"That door is stuck shut," called Hal. "C'mon, we can get in the side door." He darted around the corner of the garage and stopped in surprise. "Hey!" he exclaimed. He stared in puzzlement at the small side door, **which was secured by a padlock.**

"What's the matter, Hal?" asked Bob.

"We never lock that door unless we're going to be away a long time. Now how did . . ."

The Professor's son took out a small key ring, found the right key, and hastily unlocked the side door. Bursting inside the garage, the boys looked all around. The garage seemed empty, except for some tools and old lumber that were scattered around.

Something moved in a corner! Someone was lying tied and gagged on the floor, his eyes rolling. Grunting sounds came from him as he tried to talk through the gag.

"It's Skinny!" Bob said.

They untied the youth.

"What happened, Skinny?" Pete demanded.

Skinny Norris sat up. His face was pale and his eyes were scared. He rubbed at his wrists where the ropes had cut into him. He shivered.

"I never thought I'd be glad to see you three," Skinny said shakily. "Gosh, I'm sorry I've been trying to make trouble for you."

"I'll bet," muttered Pete. He knew that Skinny was scared and shaken now, and had little faith that the youth would be grateful **once the scare had been forgotten.**

"Skinny, tell us what happened to you!" said Jupe impatiently.

"Where have you been all night?" Bob demanded.

"Well," Skinny said nervously, "after I got away from you guys, we came out here. When we got here, he tied me up out in back somewhere! I almost fell into that barranca. You can't see it in the dark unless you know it's there. He laughed at me and said everyone fell into the barranca once before they knew it was there."

Jupiter stared at the tall youth. "Everyone falls in once, yes," he said slowly.

"Early this morning, he locked me in this garage. I've been here ever since. I was afraid to make any noise — he might have still been around. But then I heard your voices, so I tried to yell."

"Lucky for you!" Pete exclaimed.

Bob said, "Jupe? What are you thinking about?"

The stout leader of the trio was still staring at Skinny as if he saw something amazing on the youth's face. His voice seemed to tremble when he finally spoke:

"Skinny, who was it that . . ."

The side door slammed closed with a loud bang that made the boys jump in alarm.

They heard the padlock snap shut. They were locked in the darkness of the windowless garage!

"Hey!" Hal called out. "We're in here!"

There was no answer.

"Quick!" Jupiter said urgently, "look out through those cracks around the doors, and through those knotholes!"

Pete and Bob each peered out one side of the big front garage door. Jupiter found a knothole in the rear wall. Hal looked through a crack around the side door frame.

"I see someone!" Hal hissed.

The Three Investigators joined him at the side door and peeked out into the late morning sun.

"It's De Groot!" Pete whispered.

The short, heavy Dutchman stood staring at the garage, frowning. As the boys watched, he looked all around as if searching for something or someone.

"You let us out of here, De Groot!" Hal shouted.

"We know what you're after!" Bob added hotly.

De Groot scowled toward the garage. "You're all safer in there. Now be quiet! I . . ."

The Dutchman turned sharply to look

toward the big house in front, then trotted quickly out of sight into the thick chaparral behind the garage.

For a long minute nothing moved out there in the sun.

Then the boys heard someone coming, and Mr. Marechal came into sight outside the garage.

"Mr. Marechal!" Pete called out. "De Groot's out there, be careful!"

The silver-haired estate manager stared at the garage.

"He went into the brush at the rear!" Bob shouted.

Mr. Marechal turned and scanned the chaparral.

"He locked us in here. Get us out, sir!" Hal cried.

Mr. Marechal walked closer. "Is De Groot alone, boys?"

"Yes, sir," Pete called. "Skinny Norris is in here with us!"

"Norris?" Mr. Marechal said. "I see. Watch that Norris closely, boys. I don't trust him. He'll fool you all if he can!"

The silver-haired little man tried the side door. "It's padlocked out here. What about the main garage door?"

"It's stuck shut, sir," Hal explained. "But

I've got the key to the side door. I'll slide it out."

"Hey, Jupiter!" began Skinny.

"Shut up, Skinny!" hissed Jupe.

Hal took the key off his key ring, bent to slide it under the side door — and bumped hard into Jupiter. Hal lost his balance and fell over. There was a sharp metallic sound.

"The key!" Hal cried. "I lost it. Look on the floor!"

Mr. Marechal called out, "What happened, boys?"

"I dropped the key!" Hal answered. "It's dark in here. We're trying to find it on the floor."

"Hurry, boys," Mr. Marechal urged from outside.

Pete, Bob, and Hal crawled over the dark concrete floor. Skinny still sat in his corner, his scared eyes almost luminous in the dark garage. Jupiter hadn't moved since he'd bumped into Hal.

"I can't find it," Pete groaned.

"Neither can I," Bob said.

"Where could it be?" Hal moaned, feeling on the floor.

Jupiter said suddenly, "I hear a car coming, fellows."

The other boys all ran to peer out — all

except Skinny, who still sat in the corner. In the sun, Mr. Marechal looked toward the front. The boys heard a car stopping in the driveway to Professor Carswell's house. Then the little manager began to run back toward the chaparral. He disappeared into the brush, headed straight for the barranca.

"He must have seen De Groot!" Hal said.

"Oh, no!" Pete cried. "Look, fellows!"

They saw De Groot suddenly reappear at the edge of the brush, and run off in the same direction as Mr. Marechal.

The dark Dutchman had a gun!

A CRIMINAL UNMASKED

Helplessly, the boys watched through the cracks and knotholes of the garage walls. De Groot and Mr. Marechal had both disappeared. A few seconds later, Professor Carswell and the Countess came into view from the direction of the house.

"Dad!" Hal shouted.

Professor Carswell whirled about. "Hal? Where are you?"

"In the garage, Dad! We're locked in!"

Professor Carswell and the Countess hurried to the garage. The Professor unlocked the side door with his own key, and came into the garage. The boys crowded around Hal's dad and the Countess.

"How in heaven did you get locked in, boys?" Professor Carswell said.

"That De Groot locked us in," Pete explained. "Mr. Marechal would have let us out, but Hal dropped the key, and we couldn't find it. Now De Groot's chasing Mr. Marechal with a gun!"

"Armand was here?" the Countess said. "And that De Groot?"

Jupiter suddenly said in an odd voice, "You didn't know Mr. Marechal would be here, Countess? You're surprised?"

"Yes, I am surprised," the Countess said. "You see, as I just informed Professor Carswell, Mr. Marechal hasn't been at our motel since yesterday evening. He was gone all night. I don't know where or why. He told me nothing about leaving."

Professor Carswell said, "The Countess says that she saw De Groot's blue coupe at her motel early last night, too."

"Now De Groot's after him with a gun!" Pete cried.

Hal said, "If we hadn't lost the key, and if Mr. Marechal had let us out, maybe De Groot wouldn't have dared come out of hiding. We have to help Mr. Marechal!"

"No, we don't," Jupiter said. "We don't have to help Mr. Marechal, and we didn't lose the key."

The stocky leader of the Investigators moved his foot. He bent and picked up the key he had been standing on the whole time! Everyone stared at him as he held up the key to the garage.

"Jupe!" Bob said, mystified. "Why did you . . . ?"

"You were standing on the key all the time?" Pete said.

Jupiter turned to Skinny Norris in the corner. "You're quite safe now, Skinny. You can tell us who kidnapped you and locked you up here. Who you've been working for."

"He's been working with De Groot, of course!" Hal said.

"No, he hasn't," said Jupiter.

Skinny licked his lips nervously. "You're right, Jupiter. It was Mr. Marechal. He came to me that day after I'd brought Mr. James's painting to your junkyard. He hired me to pass Mr. James's paintings out that studio window so he could see if anything was hidden under the old man's paintings. I was mad at Mr. James for firing me, so I helped."

"You were working for Mr. Marechal all along?" Bob said, amazed.

"I told you none of you knew what was going on," Skinny said, with some of his old nasty sneer returning now that he was safe.

"Yes, I should have realized what you meant then," Jupiter acknowledged. "Marechal wasn't going to let us out of the garage, fellows. He was probably planning to tie us all up with Skinny! Or worse! That's why I stepped on the key. We were safer locked away from Marechal."

Pete shuddered. "Gosh, Mr. Marechal sure fooled me."

"And me," the Countess said. "Are you sure of this, Jupiter?"

"I am, Countess." Jupiter nodded firmly. "Skinny's story proves that Marechal is a dangerous character. And once you know that, a lot of puzzling details start to make sense. For instance, the police have not yet appeared in this case. Marechal said he was going to call the police when he fired us. But he didn't call them, did he?"

"No, I suppose he never did," the Countess agreed.

"Of course not," said Jupiter. "The police would have jeopardized his plans. He didn't fire us because of the danger. He wanted to get us out of his way! He had Skinny, so he didn't want us around.

"And now we know why Skinny was at your motel yesterday morning," Jupiter went on. "He was merely looking for Marechal. He ran off to avoid talking to us. But we misinterpreted his actions and thought he was trying to break in and then flee."

"See, you're not so smart after all," jeered Skinny.

Jupiter ignored him and continued. "I don't suppose, Countess, that Mr. Marechal ever went to talk to the woman who bought Joshua's statue of Venus and wouldn't sell it back?"

"Not that I know of, Jupiter," replied the Countess.

"I thought not," said Jupe. "He was always more interested in the missing paintings than in your family heirlooms. And once he heard Hal repeat Joshua's last words, he *knew* the paintings were the key."

"Key, Jupiter?" The Countess frowned. "Key to what?"

"To where old Joshua hid a lost masterpiece by François Fortunard, Countess. A supposedly destroyed painting that Mr. James says would be worth a large fortune."

"But, Jupiter," Professor Carswell objected, "how would Marechal have known that old Joshua had the masterpiece? The

Countess doesn't know. Surely she would know more about her own brother than Marechal could have."

"No, sir," Jupiter said firmly. "I am afraid that Marechal has been deceiving the Countess. You see, I made some other deductions while we were locked in the garage. I am now quite sure that it wasn't De Groot who shut us up in the adobe two days ago, and searched it so frantically. And De Groot wasn't the mysterious intruder that very first day, when Uncle Titus bought Joshua's things from you. It was Marechal! He knew about the masterpiece all the time. He came here secretly, *before* he came with the Countess, to try to get it."

"How would he have known what Joshua had?" the Countess demanded.

"He always knew, Countess," Jupiter said. "You recall Hal told us that old Joshua babbled about *tell them* and *tell 'em?* Well, he wasn't really saying either. He was actually saying *tell M.* You see? *M.* Tell *Marechal!* Because Marechal was old Joshua's partner!"

"Partner?" the Countess said. "Partner in what? Some criminal endeavor, you mean?"

"I think so, Countess. Something criminal involving the lost Fortunard masterpiece.

I'm not sure yet exactly what they were up to, but I'm sure it was something nefarious."

"I am shocked, Jupiter!" the Countess said. "We must call the police to apprehend Armand, then, before he can do more!"

"And don't forget that De Groot could still be around," added Bob. "He's involved somehow."

"I'll go and call the police at once," Professor Carswell said. "Skinny, you come with me."

"We'll come along, too," Jupe said. "I want to see the paintings again. We must solve the riddle of where the masterpiece is hidden before Marechal or De Groot does, or the police could be too late!"

A ZIG FOR A ZAG

Everyone hurried into the big house. Professor Carswell and Skinny disappeared down the hall to call the police. The other boys and the Countess went into the living room, where the twenty paintings were lined up around the walls.

"I set them up in order, Jupiter," Hal pointed out. "Number one is on the left, and number twenty all the way to the right."

They all stared at the twenty paintings of the cottage. Each one done in its different style, and each one with everything the same size except the cottage itself. The Countess, who had never seen them before, blinked in confusion.

"Why," the elegant lady said, "it looks like the house is shrinking! Quite a remarkable effect. Amazing, really!"

"Yes," Jupiter mused. "It seems that Joshua was a very skilled painter. I expect that such an effect isn't easy."

"But what does it tell us, Jupe?" Pete demanded.

"Well," the stocky leader of the trio said, "Bob suggested that perhaps something in all the pictures remains exactly the same. Such as a tree. Can anyone see something?"

They all peered at the row of paintings. One by one, they shook their heads. Everything except the cottage with its gaily striped, patched awning remained the same size, but nothing remained exactly the same in shape, color, or position.

Only Hal had an idea. "It's sort of like a microscope, or telescope, you know?" he said, staring at the paintings of the shrinking house. "I mean, as if we were focusing down through some kind of instrument onto the house."

"Focusing?" Jupiter said slowly.

"I see what Hal means," Bob said. "Sort of fixing our attention on the cottage. Telling us that the only important part of the paintings is the cottage itself."

Jupiter's eyes suddenly began to widen. He blinked rapidly at the series of paintings, and quickly took the piece of paper with Joshua Cameron's last words on it from his pocket. He studied the paper, his eyes bright with excitement.

"*Tell M.*," he read. "That means tell Marechal, I'm sure. *My paintings* and *master* mean that the clue to the hiding place of the masterpiece is in his twenty paintings. *Zig when zag* and *wrong way* mean, I think, that we are to find something that is wrong — that should zig, but that zags instead!"

Jupiter put down the paper. "So far, Joshua's message adds up to this: Tell Marechal that the key to the masterpiece is in my paintings, in something that zigs when it should zag!" He looked at them all in triumph. "And that leaves just one word of Joshua's that we haven't accounted for yet!"

They were all silent, mystified. Then Pete leaned over and looked at the paper with the words on it.

"*My canvas*," he read. "Or just *canvas*. Hal wasn't sure. But what does that tell us, Jupe?"

"Look at the twenty paintings!" Jupiter said.

They all looked.

"On the house! On the shrinking cottage itself!" Jupiter urged. "The house is so small in the last painting that almost all we can focus on is . . ."

"The porch awning!" Bob cried.

"A striped awning!" Hal said.

"A canvas awning!" Pete exclaimed.

"With patches on it, fellows," Jupiter finished. "And one of the patches has the stripes going the wrong way!"

"Stripes that zig," Bob said with awe, "when they are supposed to zag!"

"To the cottage, men!" Jupiter said.

The boys all ran out of the house and across the lawn to the cottage. The Countess was right behind them. Jupiter looked up at a large patch that was just about the size of old Joshua Cameron's paintings — a canvas patch that had been put on with the awning stripes going the wrong way!

Pete and Hal brought a ladder from the garage. Pete climbed up, took out his pocket knife, and carefully cut the heavy stitching that held the awning patch in place. The patch came off in one large piece. Pete dropped it down to Jupiter, who absentmindedly rolled it up while he stared up at the awning.

Under the patch, where there should have

been nothing, or at least only an area of damaged awning, there was another patch of plain canvas. Carefully, gently, Pete cut the four small stitches that held the plain-looking patch. It came off, revealing a perfectly undamaged area of the original awning.

"There wasn't any need for a patch here at all," Pete said.

"Bring it down and turn it over!" Jupiter said.

Pete climbed down and turned over the plain piece of canvas. They all gaped at the dazzling sight. The gorgeous colors seemed to glow in the sunlight. They looked at the great purple mountain, the blue horses, the yellow palm trees, and the red people. They had the lost masterpiece of François Fortunard!

"Bring it inside," Jupiter said.

Pete and Bob carried it gingerly inside the cottage. The Countess touched the painting almost reverently as the boys laid it on a table.

"It must be worth a king's ransom, boys," the elegant lady said. "How on earth did my poor brother get it?"

"Well, ma'am . . ." Jupiter began.

Professor Carswell came in with Skinny. "The police are on their way. I spoke to Chief

Reynolds, and . . . you found it! Where was it?"

The boys quickly explained Jupiter's solution.

"Fine work, Jupiter!" the Professor said. "Who would have thought to look under a patch in an old awning full of patches? A perfect hiding place — waterproof, safe, and close to old Joshua all the time, eh? However, I suggest you roll it up now, and handle it carefully. It could be easily damaged now that it's out in the open."

As the others watched, Bob and Pete carefully rolled the masterpiece for safekeeping and gave it to Jupiter. Skinny looked on sourly.

"Well, Countess," Professor Carswell said, smiling, "unless it turns out to be stolen, I suppose it belongs to you. A fortune!"

"Stolen?" the Countess said. "You think Joshua stole it?"

"No," Jupiter said. "I don't think it is stolen, but — "

A long shadow suddenly filled the small living room. A thin shadow with a gun! A voice chuckled:

"But now I will steal it!"

Mr. Marechal stood in the doorway with

an ugly pistol aimed at them all. The Countess glared at the silver-haired man.

"You're a despicable thief! You won't get away with this!"

"Yes, I will." Mr. Marechal smiled nastily. "Don't try to stop me, my dear Countess. I won't hesitate to use this pistol!"

The little man looked greedily at the rolled canvas in Jupiter's hand. "I congratulate you, Jupiter. You beat me to the solution of old Joshua's puzzle. Luckily, I have been watching you closely. Now . . ."

Mr. Marechal cocked his head. They all heard the distant sirens coming toward the canyon. Mr. Marechal waved his pistol.

"No more talk! Give it to me. Quickly!"

Jupiter hesitated, clutching the canvas.

"I warn you!" Mr. Marechal cried, aiming the pistol.

"Give it to him, Jupiter," Professor Carswell said.

"Hurry!" Mr. Marechal snarled.

Jupiter gulped, and held out the rolled canvas. Mr. Marechal grabbed it, waved his gun in warning, and ran out the door. As soon as he was gone, they all rushed to the windows.

"Stop him!" the Countess cried.

"No," Professor Carswell said, "it's too dangerous. Let him go."

In despair, they watched Mr. Marechal run across the lawn and disappear behind some shrubbery along the road. A moment later the yellow Mercedes raced away down the canyon. The sirens of the police came closer.

"The police will stop him!" Professor Carswell said.

"No." Jupiter shook his head. "They're looking for a blue coupe, not a yellow Mercedes."

As usual, Jupiter was right. When the police arrived a minute later, the yellow Mercedes was not with them.

JUPITER REVEALS
THE TRUTH

They all rushed out of the cottage to meet Chief Reynolds and his men. Professor Carswell quickly explained all that had happened. The Chief was upset.

"Why, we passed that yellow Mercedes," the Chief exclaimed.

"You must go after Marechal at once!" the Countess insisted. "He's a criminal! He'll escape with the masterpiece!"

"No, he won't," Jupiter said, and grinned at them all. "Luckily, you used your sirens, Chief Reynolds. They scared him so much, he never even looked at the canvas he grabbed from me."

Jupiter held up a second rolled canvas!

"This is the lost Fortunard," the First Investigator said with a triumphant laugh. "Marechal is escaping with nothing but a roll of awning canvas! I switched them on him!"

Jupiter unrolled the canvas he held, and revealed the dazzling masterpiece.

For a moment, everyone blinked at Jupiter and the magnificent painting. Then they all began to laugh. Chief Reynolds patted Jupiter on the back.

"Very good, Jupiter," the Chief beamed. "Marechal should have been more careful in dealing with you. He didn't realize your resourcefulness as we do, eh?" The Chief laughed, and told one of his men to radio in an alert for the yellow Mercedes.

"We beat him, Jupe!" Bob and Pete exclaimed together.

"Not yet, fellows," Jupiter pointed out. "We have saved the lost Fortunard from him, but he must still be apprehended."

"We'll get him easily now, Jupiter," Chief Reynolds said confidently. "If he had the painting, capturing him would be complicated. He might threaten to destroy the painting, or we might accidentally damage it. But now he won't get far — not with a roll of awning canvas!"

"There is still that De Groot to find," Professor Carswell remembered. "They are probably partners in this affair."

"Sure they are," Pete agreed. "We better still keep an eye on that masterpiece!"

"Well," the Countess said, smiling at the boys, "you young men have certainly proven yourselves to me. I do not think De Groot will get my masterpiece now. I intend to see that you boys are handsomely rewarded."

Bob and Pete blushed with pleasure at the elegant lady's praise. But Jupiter seemed to be thinking about something. The First Investigator was staring at the masterpiece.

"Chief?" Professor Carswell said. "Just whom does the painting belong to now? It would seem to be the Countess's, unless old Joshua stole it from somewhere. He did seem to think he had to hide it."

"I'm sure my poor brother didn't steal it. Poor Joshua was quite eccentric, but he wasn't a thief."

"No," Jupiter said suddenly, "I don't think the painting was stolen from anyone."

"Then I plan to present it to some fine museum," the Countess said. "Such a work of genius belongs to all the world."

"We'll have to investigate it, of course," Chief Reynolds said. "We'll hold it until then.

But if Jupiter is right, and it isn't stolen, I'm sure any museum will be grateful to you, Countess. Now — "

"Look!" the Countess suddenly cried out. "At the garage back there! It's De Groot!"

They all whirled. There was no one at the garage.

"I saw him! De Groot!" the Countess insisted. "He was at the corner of the garage with a pistol! He ran back when I called out!"

"He won't get away!" Chief Reynolds said grimly. "My men and I will go left around the house. Professor, you and the boys go to the right. If you see De Groot, try to drive him toward us. Take young Norris with you — I'll deal with him later. Countess, you watch the masterpiece."

The boys followed the Professor toward the garage. Skinny Norris went reluctantly, as if afraid of De Groot. But they saw no trace of the Dutchman. At the far side of the garage, they met Chief Reynolds and his men.

"Any sign of him?" the Chief asked.

"No," Professor Carswell said. "What could he hope to do with you and your men around?"

"I don't know," the Chief said. "It's easy to hide around here. I think we — "

"Chief!" Jupiter exclaimed all at once. "We'd better go back to the cottage. Quickly!"

"What, Jupiter?" Chief Reynolds said. "Why?"

"Hurry, sir!"

Jupiter led them all back to the front of the big house. It was Bob who saw the figures running in the driveway.

"Look! It's De Groot!"

"And the Countess!" Hal pointed. "De Groot's chasing her!"

"She's got the painting!" Pete said.

"De Groot fooled us," Professor Carswell cried. "He circled around to steal the painting, and the Countess ran with it! She's trying to reach my car!"

The police had their guns out. The Countess had almost reached Professor Carswell's car, with De Groot close behind her. Chief Reynolds fired a warning shot into the air. De Groot and the Countess stopped. The police, Professor Carswell, and the boys ran up to the pair.

"Now we've got you, De Groot!" Bob crowed.

"Thank goodness!" the Countess said. "He tried to grab the masterpiece, so I ran with it! Arrest him, Chief!"

"Yes," Chief Reynolds said. "You're under arrest, Mr. De Groot. You have the right — "

"No," Jupiter said. "Not De Groot. Arrest the Countess!"

For a moment, they were all struck dumb.

"That is a poor joke, Jupiter," the Countess said.

Jupiter shook his head. "It's not a joke, Countess. You were trying to escape with the painting. You knew that if the painting was investigated, you would never get it. In fact, you might even go to prison! De Groot was trying to stop you!"

"Nonsense," the elegant lady said. "It's my painting!"

"Yes, it is," Jupiter agreed. "Because it was Joshua's, and Joshua really had two partners — Marechal and you."

"So?" the dark-eyed De Groot said. "You know, do you? It seems I made a mistake. I should have worked with you boys instead of trying to keep you out. I underestimated you."

"Jupiter, what are you talking about?" Chief Reynolds demanded. "Who is De Groot?"

"I presume he is some kind of Dutch policeman," Jupiter said. "He has been pursuing Marechal and the Countess."

De Groot nodded. "The boy is quite right, Chief. I am a private detective from Amsterdam. I have been after Joshua Cameron and his confederates for many years. I knew of his masterpiece, and when I heard he had died here in Rocky Beach, I hurried here to prevent Marechal or the Countess from getting it."

"They were both Joshua's partners in crime," Jupiter continued. "Mr. Marechal tried to double-cross the Countess. When we defeated him, the Countess tried to get the painting by pretending to see De Groot and making us chase him. Alone, she tried to escape with it to Professor Carswell's car. But De Groot really *was* watching, and pursued her."

"Exactly," De Groot said. "Now she will go to prison!"

"Then the Fortunard is actually stolen?" the Chief said.

"No, sir, it isn't stolen," Jupiter said, "In fact, it doesn't exist — it was destroyed by the Nazis, as Mr. James said."

"But . . ." Chief Reynolds began.

"Jupiter!" Bob exclaimed. "We all can see . . ."

Jupiter smiled grimly. "You remember that old Joshua once told Hal that he was the most expensive painter in the world, but that no one knew it? Well, he was!"

"Ah," De Groot said in admiration. "So you know it all, young man? You are a most intelligent detective."

"Know what, Jupe?" Pete cried.

"That old Joshua Cameron was, indeed, a great painter. He was a master painter — of forgeries! The valuable Fortunard is a complete forgery, a fake, and that is why Marechal and the Countess wanted it — so that they could sell it to some victim."

"But," Chief Reynolds said, "De Groot just said that he came here because he knew old Joshua had a masterpiece."

"Joshua did, Chief," Jupiter said. "His own last masterpiece. A masterpiece of forgery!"

ALFRED HITCHCOCK
MISSES A CLUE

"Confound it!" Alfred Hitchcock said over the telephone. "Must I spend my existence introducing juvenile investigators?"

Bob pleaded into the phone, "Just read our report, sir. This is one of Jupiter's most brilliant cases. You'll learn a lot!"

The great director was ominously silent. "Are you suggesting, Bob Andrews, that Jupiter Jones is more intelligent than I?"

"Oh no, sir," Bob said hastily. "You could be a fine detective, I'm sure, if . . . er, I mean . . ."

"Thunderation!" There was another icy silence. "Very well, Bob Andrews, bring your report to my office. I shall read it, and I will introduce this case again — on one condition."

"What is that, sir?" Bob asked uneasily.

"That there is oné deduction I am unable to make, using the same evidence that the insufferable Jupiter had!"

Bob gulped. "I guess that's okay, sir."

"Then present yourselves at my office tomorrow!"

The next day, Bob, Pete, and Jupiter sat in Mr. Hitchcock's office. The director looked up from the Investigators' report and smiled at them smugly.

"So, the rough Mr. De Groot is a detective, while the suave Mr. Marechal and the elegant Countess prove to be criminals! Ah, how simple it would be if only we could look at people and know what they were! Has Mr. Marechal been apprehended as yet?"

"Yes, sir," Pete said, "and he and the Countess are telling everything about each other! They made a fortune for years, selling old Joshua's forged paintings to dupes in Europe. A year ago they were sent to jail for a short time. Old Joshua escaped the police and fled to America with his last masterpiece. So —"

"Stop!" Mr. Hitchcock cried. "I will now exhibit my own deductions. Being in prison, they could not act on Professor Carswell's letter relating Joshua's death until their release. Marechal was released a week before the Countess, and came to Rocky Beach at once. He intended to double-cross the Countess by getting the forged masterpiece first. But he failed to locate it, injured his leg in the barranca, and so returned to Europe to recover and rejoined the Countess."

"Those were my conclusions," Jupiter agreed.

"De Groot learned of Joshua's demise, and followed the pair here. As soon as he realized Marechal was interested in Skinny Norris, he assumed that the con man would try to sell the master forgery to the Norrises. Therefore he tapped their phone, hoping that he could follow Marechal's progress and catch him in the act."

Jupiter nodded.

Mr. Hitchcock beamed confidently. "Old Joshua had hidden his masterpiece of forgery, to keep it from prying eyes such as young Hal's. Then he had to devise some means of letting his confederates know where the masterpiece was, in case anything happened to him. I presume that he did not dare to write to them about it. So he painted twenty numbered pictures of a shrinking house. Then, ironically, he betrayed his secret to others by babbling a message to Marechal before his death.

"As soon as Marechal learned of the existence of the paintings, he knew they would lead him to the master forgery. Old Joshua's last words confirmed that they were the key — though Marechal never quite understood the whole message. After Skinny appeared with the one painting, Marechal contacted him. Skinny, having been fired, foolishly fell in with the plot to pass the paintings out the window of Mr. James's studio so that Marechal could examine them."

"Marechal thought the forgery might be *under* one of the paintings, just as I did," Jupiter said.

"A natural conclusion, if erroneous," Mr. Hitchcock said. "But Marechal continued to search as well, and it was he who locked you in the adobe. Then Skinny was caught in the studio, and Marechal had to abduct him to save himself. Luckily, when you were in the garage, you guessed Marechal was a villain in time to prevent his capturing all of you — if not doing worse! De Groot, of course, had **locked you all in the garage for your safety!**

Incidentally, I presume that De Groot's limp, which led you wrong, is some old injury?"

"Yes, sir," Bob said, "he's had it for years."

Mr. Hitchcock nodded. "Finding the masterpiece was excellent reasoning, but you have explained that in your report. Then, Jupiter, you deduced that old Joshua and Marechal were art forgers. What you did not know at that point was the Countess's role. You became suspicious of the Countess when she claimed to have seen Mr. De Groot by the garage. As far as you knew, the Countess had never met him while she was in Rocky Beach. Obviously she had run into him before. Since De Groot had been following Marechal from the beginning, and since he had done nothing after all except try to scare you away from Marechal, it was probable that he was some sort of policeman. When he chased the Countess at the finish, it became clear that she, too, must have been a confederate of old Joshua's, and was trying to grab the fake Fortunard!"

Jupiter sighed. "That is how I reasoned, yes."

"But," Pete said eagerly, "how did Jupe guess that old Joshua was a forger at all, Mr. Hitchcock?"

"Why, that is quite clear, Peter. There was, of course, old Joshua's hint to Hal about being expensive but no one knowing it. Plus Mr. James telling you that old Joshua was a fine painter who had imitated twenty different styles. Who could paint so well, in so many styles, and remain totally unknown? A master forger!"

"That's just how I figured it out, sir," Jupiter agreed.

"Which ends the case," the famous director beamed, "and, since I have understood all, I am relieved of an introduction!"

Bob was glum. "I guess so, sir."

"Excellent," Mr. Hitchcock declared. "Then may I inquire as to the ultimate fate of the principal characters in this case?"

"Well," answered Jupiter, "Marechal has already been charged with abducting Skinny Norris, and will certainly go to jail here for it. The Countess is not involved in that charge, but the police are holding her in custody until the European officials decide what to do about her — put her in jail for her past crimes, probably. De Groot has gone back to Amsterdam. His client, you know, was a wealthy former victim of the forgery gang who wanted them busted up for good.

The man was not at all satisfied when the Countess and Marechal went to jail for only a year and Joshua Cameron escaped. He should be happy now."

Mr. Hitchcock nodded. "And what will be the disposition of the forged masterpiece?"

"Technically, it does belong to the Countess," said Jupe. "But it's worthless to her now. Since she can't do business with it, she doesn't want it. She has given it to Professor Carswell in payment of Joshua's debts. It will bring much more than that. A collector of forgeries has already offered a large sum. With the money, Professor Carswell and Hal will restore their fine old house and the adobe."

"People are already trying to buy old Joshua's twenty paintings," Bob said. "Mr. James has them back now."

"And what of Skinny Norris?"

"Skinny was just stupid, as usual," Jupiter said. "The police won't charge him, but his parents have sent him back to school for the summer."

"Good," Mr. Hitchcock said. "Now, I am busy, and if —"

"Er, Mr. Hitchcock," Pete said suddenly. "I think there's one deduction you haven't explained — how Jupe knew, when De Groot locked us in the garage and looked guilty, that it was really Mr. Marechal who was guilty? That was the real turning point."

"What? Why . . ."

"Skinny had been too scared to tell us yet," Bob pointed out quickly. "He might never have talked if Jupe hadn't guessed!"

Mr. Hitchcock studied the boys' report, flipping pages. "Aha!" he exclaimed. "Jupiter knew Marechal was guilty when he realized that *Tell them* meant *tell M.!*"

"No!" said Jupiter, laughing. "That came later. While we were in the garage, Skinny said something that let me know Marechal was the one."

"Skinny said . . . he said . . ." The director glared at the report, then glared at the boys. "Well, confound it, what *did* Skinny say that told you De Groot was innocent, and Marechal was the crook?"

Jupiter grinned. "Skinny said that his abductor had laughingly observed that everyone fell into the barranca once, before he knew it was there."

"Yes, yes! Go on! Tell me!" said Mr. Hitchcock impatiently.

"De Groot fell into the barranca that night at the adobe," Jupiter said simply.

Mr. Hitchcock groaned. "Of course! De

Groot wouldn't have fallen if he had known the barranca was there! That meant that De Groot couldn't have locked you in the adobe earlier, and he couldn't have been the mysterious intruder of the first day, despite his limp. Once you realized that, then the intruder almost had to be Mr. Marechal! Thunderation, but you've done it!"

"All along, I thought something seemed wrong that night at the adobe," added Jupe smugly.

The great director groaned again. "Monstrous! But I have failed, I missed a clue, and I must introduce this case!"

"Thank you, sir!" Bob exclaimed.

"We really appreciate it, sir," Pete enthused.

"And, as a consolation, Mr. Hitchcock," Jupiter said with a smile, producing a painting from the floor, "we have asked Mr. James to let you have one of the paintings of the shrinking house."

"Sometimes," Mr. Hitchcock said as he took the painting, "you young schemers are as devious as your villains! Be off!"

The boys hastily left the office. Behind them, Mr. Hitchcock looked at the painting by old Joshua Cameron, the master forger of art, and laughed.